About the Author

Jon-Jon was born Jon Stephen Jones in the South Midlands, UK and now lives in central London. He has always had a love of reading and particularly enjoys the Adventure Classics as well as Childrens.

As well as Victorian Adventure Stories Jon-Jon has also released his debut novel Tiger! Tiger! Tiger!

Future titles include the Tigerian, a children's book series entitled Aaron the Alien, a Children's novel called The Jellyset Kid and a travel series called The Jaunts of Jon-Jon as well as poetry and a blog.

For more information on Jon-Jon and Tiger! Tiger! Tiger! please visit:

www.Jon-Jon.co.uk

For his Aaron the Alien series visit

www.AarontheAlien.com

<u>In memory of Mike Marwick 1970-2018</u>

To Stay or Not to Tay

Dedicated to the 75 souls who lost their lives on 28th December 1879 in the Tay Bridge disaster.

The Magic Circle

A commemorative story to mark 150 years of the London (Tube) Underground.

Victorian Adventure Stories

Copyright Notice

This book is copyright material and must not be copied, reproduced, transferred, distributed, leased, licensed or publicly performed or used in any way except as specifically permitted in writing by the author, as allowed under terms and conditions under which it was purchased or as strictly permitted by applicable copyright law. Any unauthorised distribution or use of this text may be a direct infringement of the author's rights and those responsible maybe liable in law accordingly.

The moral right of Jon Stephen Jones – Jon-Jon to be identified as the author of this work has been asserted in accordance with the Copyright, Designs & Patents Act 1988

Copyright © 2018 Jon Stephen Jones – Jon-Jon
All Rights Reserved

This book is a work of fiction. Names, characters, places and incidents are either a product of the authors imagination or used fictitiously. Any resemblance to actual people living or dead, events or locales is entirely coincidental.

Ebooks are not transferable.

Library of Congress Control Number

Victorian Adventure Stories
TXU002089271

Cover by
www.damonza.com

VICTORIAN ADVENTURE STORIES

Contents

Henchman 1

The Cats of Kensington Mews 31

Swing II 43

A Hebridian Adventure 53

The Magic Circle 77

Bleeding Chips 87

A Great Exhibition 115

Such Fun 127

The Box 139

Next of Kin 159

To Stay or Not to Tay 175

Henchman

'*I don't want this life no more, you understand me, I don't want it Craig.*' John said punching him again in the stomach.

Craig buckled over. 'You can't leave John, he won't let you and you know that.'

John walked over and helped Craig up. 'Well you better get the bleedin message through to em' all hadn't you? I'm out of this game, it's not what I want anymore, it will only end up with me dangling from a rope. I got into this game only for the money, I'm a low level enforcer for the gang that is all and I am easily replaced.'

'You became too good John. The Doctor sees you as a valuable asset now. You have completed every task that we have given you, you have saved us from arrest and fought when we have been heavily outnumbered and won. You're better than good, you're brilliant, you're a natural thug, you're a villain, it's in your blood.'

'Don't say that to me Craig.' said John looking away.

'Do you know what the dreaded doctor said or should I say instructed? He said that when we're out on assignment you should be listened to at all costs and that if you give an instruction we are to obey it. I am risking reprisals by even telling you this.'

'That makes no sense Craig, why would he do that?'

'I don't know. The doctor never fully reveals his plans, you know that, but it is obvious that you are going to go a long way… it is either a test or-' Craig paused mid sentence in deep thought. 'Or he knew you were planning to leave the gang. Who did you tell John?'

'No-one. You were the first to know and I informed the rest of the gang the following night.'

'There must be some other purpose then.'

'It matters not Craig I am out and that is the end of the story.'

'Don't be a fool, if you carry on trying to leave you will be filled with lead long before you ever have to worry about a rope. John, the doctor doesn't leave loose ends.'

'Craig, I have known you the longest and you are the closest to me which is why you only got punches, but if you try and follow me again I may not be so gentle, friend or not.'

'I hope I won't have to, but we all have to obey him John and you are forewarned of the consequences if you don't.'

'We will see.'

Craig bent down and picked his cap up from the floor. 'Hopefully we won't have to, look, I will buy you some time, I will say that you are thinking about it and that you will attend the meeting on Thursday. Be there John, for Christ's sake, be there.

John with his huge baldhead and cruel mouth had a two-man chest that caused him to walk like a bear through an abandoned forest. The gang tattoos on his forearms looked like some ill conceived, angry Rorschach. An empty brougham rattled past and John briefly considered hailing for it, but he believed that Craig was no longer following him.

He continued walking, a few streets later he turned into a plusher neighbourhood, at the end of this street was a pub that he used to frequent during a quiet period in his life, a time when violence and skulduggery was not a natural part of the day's proceedings.

John put the encounter with Craig out his mind and allowed the fresh evening air to reinvigorate him, but his hard-soled shoes offered no comfort against the bitter cobblestones. He approached *the Tiger's Tooth* public house. The pub was half-full, gentlemen in their waistcoats smoked in an industrious fashion. There were a few women as well, an occurrence that had been became more frequent over recent years, John paid no attention it didn't bother him.

John did not recognise anyone, he was hopeful of a familiar face but even the staff had changed, there was a new landlord, some chap with a shiny black beard. John ordered a beer and sat at the bar, he swiftly drunk it and ordered another. On his fourth beer, an attractive young woman came and sat next him.

John looked at her closely she had on a nice blue skirt with a white blouse, her hair was long and brown but she wore it tied up, the skin on her face was smooth although on closer inspection he surmised she was older than she initially appeared. She had an infectious smile and earlobes just a little longer than they should be.

'Do you mind sir?' she asked.

John could see there were plenty of other places to sit; he became slightly suspicious. 'Not at all.'

'Forgive me it may not seem very lady like but I enjoy sitting at the bar and it is not illegal so I shall do as I wish.'

John smiled at her feistiness. 'Here alone?'

'Yes, afraid so, are you sir?'

'Why did you sit next to me there are plenty of other stools available?'

'If my presence offends you I shall remove myself from it.' she said stepping off the bar-stool.

'That's not what I meant; it just seemed a trifle odd is all.'

'There is nothing a trifle odd about a woman sitting next to a man, we are both on our own, it also makes me appear-'

'Less conspicuous?' John said finishing her sentence for her.

'Yes, you make me less conspicuous, not that I need you to, it is just that ... well to be frank you look like you have the world on your shoulders.'

'Didn't mean to be rude. Trust me madam you would not want to associate with my sort.'

'And why is that?' she asked sitting back on the stool ensuring her skirt did not hitch up.

'Because I'm not your sort.'

'*Ooh forgive me sir*, but all you do is to entice me all the more.'

'I may be smartly dressed myself but I'm a ...'

'Ruffian?'

'Yes, in your world I suppose you would class me as ruffian.'

'My world, so just what exactly is my world?'

John took a swig of his beer holding onto his glass tighter than usual. Beating men to death was never a problem; talking to a lady however ...

'You know, you're a demure lady obviously of some standing, you have no place in the world I live in.'

The woman burst out laughing.

'Really? So does this ruffian have a name?'

John sat there and debated lying to her but he was too attracted to her. He was beginning to think that the feeling maybe reciprocated. Yet how could he bring her into his world?

'John.' he blurted out before he could finish making his decision.

'My name is Emily Tempsford pleased to make your acquaintance.' she replied offering her lace covered hand.

John kissed it as gently as he could.

'And what is your surname? I gave you mine?'

Now this John would lie about if only to protect her. 'John Felmersham.'

'So how rough are we talking?'

John looked at her quizzically, 'I beg your pardon?'

'You informed me you were a ruffian, how rough?'

'Too rough for you.'

'That will not suffice. Do you hurt people? Get into pub fights? Underground boxing perhaps?'

'Gangs.' John said solemnly.

'Go on, do not stop there.' she said with an air of authority that can only come from a true lady.

'The medics.' John replied in a quiet tone.

'*The Medics!* They are the most feared gang in London.'

'And the biggest. I warned you that you wouldn't want to know.'

Emily composed herself again. 'It has not changed anything why should it affect me?'

'I should not have told you that.' John began to realise the great power she was already wielding over him, he felt helpless against her as if he were some trapped animal being pulled out of a well. 'I am tired of the gang life and no longer wish to be part of our evil ways. The trouble is when you join the gang you swear never to leave it 'on pain of death' and it does literally mean that. The doctor is not a forgiving man.'

'Oh yes, he is called the Dreaded Doctor isn't he?'

'Yes, but those who work just call him the doctor.'

'He is the most feared man in London the stuff I have read about him and his gang in the papers. Have you ever seen him?'

'No. No one sees him and lives to tell the tale that is his genius. Every order or command is passed down we do not even know whether he is tall or short. He sent someone to warn me tonight, but this was a friendly warning. Next time more men will come or I might just be randomly shot dead.'

'None of this scares you?'

'No. I don't know why. I guess I have lived this lifestyle one night too long.'

'I would not agree with that; can't the doctor be bartered with?'

'No. There is no point, that's the rules and to be fair I agreed to them.'

'Please do not justify such a heinous man or gang. I suspect it is your conscience that is protesting.'

'Maybe, but I had no qualms in carrying out his orders. So it can't affect me that much.'

'What will happen next?' said Emily softly touching John's hand for the briefest of moments.

'There is a meeting on Thursday evening if I am not there then I figure that will be the last line crossed.'

John could feel her soft brown eyes examining his face looking for expression.

'Would you be interested in courting me?'

John nearly choked on his beer. He felt perplexed and slightly embarrassed.

'Could you repeat that please?' asked John.

'No I jolly well cannot. You heard me perfectly well, I warned you I can look after myself and I will consider it most rude if you do not provide me with an answer.'

'Yes, the answer is most certainly yes.' said John looking away. It had been many years since he had flushed red with embarrassment.

'Excellent. What time is your meeting on Thursday evening?'

'Seven-thirty.'

'Ok, here is my proposal I will be here sitting at this bar at seven-thirty on Thursday evening. You have a choice you can go back to your gang or you can come here and start courting a beautiful woman.' she smiled with a slight coquettishness.

John felt his face turning red again; he felt alarmingly hot all of a sudden.

'I will leave that with you then.' Emily said getting up from her bar-stool.

John got up, 'I will walk you out as I was going after this one anyway.'

'Do not lie to me John it is not very appealing.'

John sniggered to himself. 'You have me there I was staying until the barrel is dry.'

'I know. See you Thursday perhaps.' John thought for a moment that she was going to lean forward and kiss him. He watched as she masterfully hung her umbrella on her arm and walked out in a demure yet confident fashion.

John finished the rest of the evening in the pub as promised. Somewhere deep in the recesses of his stone cold heart this woman had started looking for fissures. Emily was in his subconscious, in his hopes, in his dreams.

A brief recollection of stumbling home, ransacking the pantry, he could definitely remember that. John got some beer as he was thirsty; he briefly wondered whether water would ever be safe enough to drink. He had a strip wash and clothed himself still wet.

In the parlour he lit a pipe and had his first smoke of the day. Cigarettes were his usual fixture on the street but for some reason he had grown an affinity for a pipe first thing in the morning. He grabbed yesterday's paper off the table and sat down, it was easier to steal a paper in the afternoon and read it the next day. He read a headline about the police stepping up their efforts to bring down the so-called *medics* gang, but particularly to uncover the identity of the Dreaded Doctor. John laughed to himself and wondered whether the Dreaded Doctor had run the article himself.

Within the hour, John was ready to go about his day's business, he walked to the door and stopped as the fresh air hit him. Where was he going? What was he going to do? His autopilot had him walking out the door to collect his rounds on behalf of the doctor, he had followed his instinct, he had left the gang but had not counted on what to do with his days, how would he earn money?

John decided to go for a stroll anyway. He entered Hyde Park and slowly meandered his way around the serpentine. For the first time he questioned his life, his decisions, what calamity had he brought upon himself? He reasoned that it was not his fault, an orphan raised in a workhouse, what chance did he have? The niggling spectre of doubt and reason bore its ugly head to the surface of his conscience. He could have turned his talents to many other things, but now he was bound by what he had sown.

He knew the doctor would kill him without a thought, but there was some honour in what he was trying to do, could even the cruelest villain somehow be reasoned with? He sat down and with his tinder lit a cigarette, the grass was still damp and he could feel the water seeping through his trousers. The fog was dispersing but mist still hung over the serpentine. Mixed with the cold air smoke billowed out of him like a chimney stack.

Was he really going to walk himself straight into the arms of death and take on this Doctor? Perhaps he could take them all out, go underground and kill them one by one, if he could survive for long enough.

His cigarette was quickly finished as he put it out she came into his mind, was this a sign? Was God really there encouraging him to leave the gang, to reward him or perhaps to punish him? He closed the door of his heart as if she was a bothersome salesman. There could be no such factor in such a momentous decision; she would have to be killed off in his mind until he had reached a decision.

This thought galvanised him back into action. Partly out of curiosity and partly to facilitate his decision John decided to spy on his own round, to see who was making them in his absence.

He was soon in the back alleys of London and moved through them like a rat in a maze. He pulled out his expensive silver pocket watch and briefly recalled the man that he had stole it from. Behind the angry facade of crime and violence you are reminded, to the point of torture, who you really are. Coming to the end of an alley he stopped behind some discarded wooden crates.

Across the street was *The Leopard's Paw*, this pub was on his collection rounds. The timing should be perfect and he wondered whom the Doctor would send? John normally did the rounds alone but sometimes Craig would accompany him.

John had struck quite a bizarre relationship with the landlord of the pub. He had initially resisted, but after a few weeks he gave up and started paying. As the months passed, the landlord seemed to forget that it was a protection racket and just treated it as if he was paying a beer supplier, occasionally John would even be offered a drink. On occasion John felt sorry for him and nearly let him off a few times but he knew the doctor would never allow it and he certainly wasn't paying for it.

He did not have to wait long. He kept half of his body behind the crates so he could lean back should one of them by perchance look across the street. John could smell the strong, stagnant urine stains from the previous night and was trying his best not to wretch. Craig came sauntering out of a side alley with three others with him. John laughed at the sight of four people going to do what he did on his own.

They all marched into the pub pulling their caps slightly down as if it made a difference. John waited a few minutes, he realised he was tapping his feet in impatience. Craig violently came crashing out of the door, then two more of the gang did and the fourth was thrown to the floor. The landlord came out of the pub and a big guy who John assumed to be a drinker.

Another man came out and instantly spotted a bobby wondering down the street towards them. The policeman looked up just as Craig was throwing a punch with a knuckle duster. The loud shrill of a policeman's whistle rang through the still morning. The bobby started running toward the group. John heard another whistle blast right behind him; he turned and saw a peeler running straight towards him. As he ran past John stuck his foot out, the policeman went airborne slamming hard into the cobblestones upon his landing.

'Sorry sir, apologies, I am so sorry, I did not see you there.'

The policeman got up, clearly bruised, he groaned as he got up from the pavement. John walked swiftly back down the alley and into an unlocked back door of a shop unit. He stood there encompassed in the musty aroma of an old store room. John listened at the door and quickly realised that the policeman was not looking for him, he walked back into the alley and out into the street. It was evident that a large fight had broken out but all of the gang had already left the scene already. John walked across the street to the landlord.

'*You bleedin idiot; you know they will be back.*'

The landlord gulped hard and nervously twiddled his moustache. 'John where did you come from? I thought you had left.'

'I have Ricky.' John replied.

'What you left the gang, you are part of this mob are you?' asked a policeman wiping blood from his mouth and then stepping forward. His colleague grabbed his arm firmly and pulled him back away from john, his face full of recognition and fear as he did so.

The big guy who had helped the landlord out was standing there his arms folded with a lump forming on the side of his face.

John looked him straight in his eyes. 'I suggest you walk away and stay away, don't ever come back to this tavern, or this part of town, I am warning you the Dreaded Doctor will be looking for you tonight.'

The man's face turned pale he ran back in the pub and grabbed his jacket and after nodding to the landlord he jumped into the first hansom he could find.

'Why did you do it Ricky?'

'Dunno, my regular here saw what was going on, got up and clobbered one of them, I just got carried away, I mean I have tolerated it John but it ain't right is it?'

'It is what is Ricky, I can't protect you I have left the gang now, I'm considered a traitor.'

'Come and work for me John, run the pub with me?'

'Don't think so and best you don't open tonight.'

'Don't worry a few of us will be down here nobody hits a copper and gets away with it.' one of the policeman said tending to the wound on his mouth.

John smiled mischievously. 'That person will not go unpunished I assure you. We are under strict instructions never to strike a policeman, I suggest you take heed of your colleague and forget all about this, you will likely disappear if you push it and before you ask, I do not know who the Dreaded Doctor is.'

The other policeman yanked his arm and with that they left, John heard him calling his friend a damned fool.

The punters were starting to move away from the windows in the pub.

'Good luck Rick.' said John placing his hand gently on Rick's shoulder.

John wondered off back toward Hyde park as if on auto pilot. The incident bothered him; his rounds were for the most part peaceful as the gang was so powerful and so well known. Its leader, the diabolical genius had kept the whole of London in shape for years. Bloodshed would now be spilt, it was unstoppable, the only realistic hope for the Good Samaritan was to leave London immediately. That wouldn't happen he knew it. He would probably stay inside for a couple of days and then come out thinking everything is fine, within a couple of weeks he would probably be back in *The Leopard's Paw*.

The park was becoming congested as the winter sun became pleasant enough to warrant the removal of overcoats. He continued his perambulation thinking about the meeting he was supposed to attend the next night. It was too late now, he had left the gang, he would be considered untrustworthy and weak. If he was allowed to live at all, he would be utilised for every nefarious deed the doctor required then he would be executed.

This fact was inevitable, there was no question or debate. He was strolling through the winter sun surmising choices when there was not a choice to consider. Emily crept back into his heart again.

A glimmer of excitement leapt out of his soul and into his eyes. Yes, he would court her and if he fell in love then he would kill them all without compunction. If life was to be short then he was going to live it on his own terms and if blood was going to be spilt then he was going to be the spiller of it. Realising that he had made up his mind he decided to retire early to his rooms and drink. Maybe read the paper in front of a roaring fire.

Thursday arrived like any other morning with John strip washing in the bathroom.

He thought about the day ahead, there would be no peril until the time of the meeting and he did not show up. John would be at his pub that he had kept purposefully secret, it was like his safe house, a place where he could seek sanctuary. He would be safe there and it was unlikely they would come looking for him on the same night. The Dreaded Doctor would wait like a Black Widow Spider cautiously planning its next meal, spinning a web of fine silk, ensuring that every strand entrapped only the intended while warning him of danger and providing a thousand escape routes.

In all likelihood it would happen in a couple of days, he would be kidnapped and then made an example of in some horrendous fashion. John leant on the bathroom sink and looked into the mirror. He had to try and think how to get the upper hand or lead them to him in a way that he could control.

He considered leverage but it was not an option, the doctor even had contingency plans for contingency plans, the only way he could get any type of leverage would be to ... to find the doctor and unmask him, once and for all.

John decided this was the plan to follow. He spent the day running errands and making enquiries through low-level enforcers and subsidiary gangs that were connected to the medics. They were not all connected by choice.

At teatime John returned home and armed himself, he took his gun, knuckleduster and had a small iron bar in his trousers. When the time came around John headed to the pub. Even in the dank gas lit gloom of *The Tiger's Tooth,* she seemed to glow. John took off his bowler as her eyes caught sight of him.

'You picked me, are you sure it is the right decision?'

'You are the decision I want even if I only have a few days to live.'

'You are the sweetest.' she said getting up and gently stroking his face.

John recoiled just for a second as he was not used to being touched but then he accepted her warm gentle hand. John pulled up the stool next to hers and ordered two beers. They looked at each other.

'Does it not bother you that you yourself maybe in peril.' John enquired.

'Myself, I never gave much thought to it; they would not dare hurt a lady surely?'

'They are capable of anything I warn you; I must also confess to you that I did not come alone tonight.'

'Oh.' she replied looking over his shoulder at the doorway.

'Not in that sense.' he replied showing her the gun tucked in his black trousers whilst at the same time questioning himself as to why he was doing so.

She looked slightly nervous. 'Oh I see ...' she said turning to her drink; her hand beginning to tremble slightly.

'The door's there.' said John pointing.

'Did I say I was ready to leave?' she said looking straight at him.

John was amazed at her spirit he was falling in love with her rapidly but tried hard to ignore the feeling. He then remembered when he first met her the way she challenged society by sitting at the bar on her own. John burst out in a raucous laugh.

'You laugh at me?' she asked, her fine, silky lips thinning as she did so.

'Only at your wonderful soul, you are quite a woman, I should set *you* on the gang.'

'Oh you are a silly man, I think that's why I like you there is so much more to you than you let people see, I can tell.'

John not knowing what to say took a sip of his drink.

They began to talk. Emily explained that she had came from a relatively wealthy background and as such could not see any reason why she should settle for the first suitor of her father's choosing, whilst she was sad at his sudden passing, she was also quite relieved as it allowed her freedom to explore the world of men for herself.

John explained about his rough and poor beginnings, how he grew up in the street and got into street fighting to earn money. How he became a gang member and then leader of a gang that was incorporated into the medics after he received a considerable lump sum of cash. He did not disclose this cash to the rest of the gang and surmised that this would be key information in turning his old crew against him. The time passed quickly and before they knew it the landlord was asking everybody to finish their drinks.

'So are you going to walk this lady home then?' she asked standing up abruptly as if expectant of servitude.

'Uh ... yes of course it would be an honour.' said John.

'Just to my door mind. I am quite capable of finding my bed by myself.'

John's cheeks flushed bright red. 'The thought never crossed my mind, how could I think so little of you.'

Emily burst out laughing watching this giant thug of a man melt into a little puppy dog.

'I'm teasing. It is very kind of you.' she said.

'I understand you perfectly well.' replied John.

'Good, then I will be expecting a kiss at the end of our late night walk.'

'Whatever the lady requires.' said John putting his hands gruffly in his pockets trying to avoid yet another flush of embarrassment.

The last ones to walk out of the public house, they stepped out into the cold air, before john could even think she had put her arms through this. John for the first time started to feel a bit nervous about her safety.

They turned a corner and started walking down an alley. All he heard was her scream his name like a wild *banshee*, the sudden immense pain, a moment of blackness. Had he fallen through some cellar door into some kind of torture device? No, he had caught an image, a boot, definitely a man's boot.

He tried to come back to his senses as quick as he could, a blow to the back of the head had knocked him out and he was now being pummelled into oblivion. John attempted to unleash a punch but he couldn't, kicks and punches were too quickly replaced by the next volley. Where was his girl and what were they going to do her? '*Kill them, kill them all.*' he screamed to himself inside his head but it was time to say goodnight as the land of darkness won over his senses.

Death what a strange sensation, no sound, nothing but stillness. Yet how could anything be sensed if he was dead, he couldn't be dead could he? John tried to move and pain shot through him like a defibrillator awaking a corpse. He opened his eye, the other would not open as it was too swollen, the side of his face hurt like hell.

As the seconds ticked by so his level of pain increased he felt it in his arms, legs, torso, face and head, even his testicles hurt. They had beaten him until he was nearly dead, he had not expected them to come at him so soon and how did they know where he was? Wait, Emily, where was she? He sat up and screamed.

'*Emily.*'

'I have been informed to tell you that she is fine, she was allowed to walk home unharmed and at the moment she is not part of this.'

'Who are you?' John asked making out the figure of a blonde lady. She gently pushed him back down to a lying position John winced as the pain once again reached a crescendo through his body.

'I have been paid very good money to look after you. I am a nurse on private hire.'

'Who hired you? *As if I don't know.*' John muttered the last part to himself.

'It was a very well dressed educated man, he paid me three months salary for one weeks work, but there are strict conditions. I am not to tell you any other details except to inform you that Emily has not been harmed and will not be for now. You will not be attacked again at least not until you recover, but it would be in your best interest to stay here in your house until then. Anything you want will be brought to you including alcohol, tobacco and other luxuries, you can order what you want and you shall not be charged, you are to consider this a professional courtesy.'

John could not help but snigger at this last sentence.

'Before you ask I am not allowed to divulge anything about myself other than to tell you that I have been hired and I am a fully qualified trained nurse.'

John remained silent and thought for a minute, he believed her, it was the fiendish sort of game the doctor would enjoy playing.

'Thank you.' he said in a broken voice and with that slipped back into unconsciousness.

The doctor was none other than Jack the Ripper, he was bullet-proof and John could not kill him. Crowds of people followed John through the streets of London jeering at him as he could not slay the beast, suddenly it was night and the beast sprung out of a foggy lane at him, nothing but a giant silhouette of the devil himself in a cloak and top hat. John awoke panting heavily.

The dream had shaken him but he knew he had to gather his senses. Emily's details, he didn't know where she lived or how to contact her. He had to find her as soon as he could leave the house.

The nurse came in everyday, cooked him meals and brought whatever shopping he required. It was not long until he was out of bed, John was pleased to discover that essentially he was just bruised all over his body, initially he thought they had broken all his limbs.

He was soon walking about and with each day he could move a bit more, his other eye opened and the swelling disappeared, by the end of the week he was working out, most his body was now a disgusting yellow.

'This is my last day. I have been told to inform you that as of dawn you are free to roam the city as you please.' said the Nurse.

'Until what is supposed to happen next.' replied John wondering both his fate and hers.

'I assure you John that is all I was told to say and all I was told. I will not scoff at money that will provide for my family so well.'

'Fair enough, let me give you some more then as I have plenty as well.'

'That is not required John, I have been paid more than my fair that shall suffice for me.'

'Well, thank you then.'

'Accepted. I shall never see you again John of that I have been assured so all that remains for me to say is God Bless.' the nurse gave a shallow courtesy with her long dress and left the house.

'God Bless you too.' said John replaying the sentence in his head, '*I will never see you again*' – was that a threat?

John had plenty of whisky, beer, brandy and enough smoke for a month, he had taken full advantage of the doctor's generosity. He cleaned his house from top to bottom and double-checked all his secret hidey-holes for cash and weapons. Everything was there, he was expecting everything to be gone, why wasn't he cleaned out? Some of his stashes were easy to find, they had to be in case he needed them quickly. Outside in the entrance hall on a little table John discovered his baton, gun, knuckle-duster and the wad of notes he had in his pocket, straight away John guessed there wasn't a ha'penny missing.

He cooked himself some lamb, placed his tobacco and bottle of whiskey by the fire and settled in for the night. His mind turned to Emily and how could he find her, the first place had to be *the Tiger's Tooth*, logic dictated it. She must be worried.

Inebriated dreams of her soft lips carried him away into oblivion. John awoke the next morning and had a soothing warm bath that seemed to heal both his wounds and hangover. Then he shaved and dressed in black trousers, white shirt and a brown waistcoat. He intended to find her no matter what and if he did he wanted to look appropriate.

He picked up his money and weapons up off the table but changed the gun for one that he had well hidden just in case it had been tampered with. When he was fully satisfied he walked out of the door. John instinctively stopped to look around, the thought occurred to him that it might have all been to kill him as soon as he stepped outside of his house, the doctor had been known to play such fiendish games before. The cobbled lane was devoid of life and glistened with the moisture of winter.

After a housebound week of silence, the noisy racket of London was welcome, the constant chatter, clarence wheels growling, inexplicable bangs and thuds and the clopping of canes and hooves. He strolled slowly back to *the*

Tiger's Tooth where he had met Emily. The front door was wide open and the landlord was behind the bar.

'Good day sir I was wondering if I would see you again. *Good God, have you got Jaundice or something? You have turned yellow.'*

John gave him a straight stare. 'I had an accident.'

The landlord stroked his black beard as if contemplating what to say. 'Well, sorry to hear that, the good news is that I have something for you.'

The landlord leant under the bar. John dived his hand into his coat firmly gripping the handle of his revolver.

'Here.' the landlord said pulling out an envelope.

John briefly smiled but quickly retained his emotions.

'Thanks Landlord, get us both a drink will you.' John said giving him some money.

'Thank you, take a stool. Same as last time?'

'Yes.'

John opened the envelope and as he did so Emily's sweet perfume wafted into his senses like a sirens call. He unfolded the square of paper inside:

Same place, same time?

John realised today was Thursday, exactly one week since he had last met Emily, she wanted to meet him tonight.

John felt charged and impulsive, he gulped down his beer, thanked the landlord for keeping the letter and tipping him generously marched out the door with determination in his step. He walked through the streets briskly and despite his aches and pains adrenaline surged through him like a stampede of fleeing gazelle.

After half an hour's walk he rounded the corner into a small circus; up ahead was a factory that dealt in second hand furniture. This was the headquarters of the notorious medics and in its warren of corridors and attics hid the spider, the Dreaded Doctor himself.

As John approached the gates he was astonished to see a large poster nailed up with four industrial sized nails, it read:

Not Today John!

John took off his hat and rubbed his head, he was surprised to find himself so easily expected. The gates were chained up, he stood there for a minute and lit a cigarette. He paced around outside the gates ensuring he could be seen from the factory windows, when his cigarette got down to the last drags, he flicked the butt away violently whilst staring at the windows. John knew there was always somebody watching.

He got back to *the Tiger's Tooth* for seven thirty, half an hour before they were supposed to meet, he opened the door and saw Emily there sitting at the bar with a drink already in front of her.

She was wearing a particularly fetching green dress and matching hat. A green umbrella hung gently from her arm. Her beautiful brown eyes lit up wide when she saw him, she got off the stall and ran to John, hugged him then kissed him. John winced as she gripped him tight. She apologised and eased off. John pulled her back and kissed her passionately, the pub was rather full and he heard the landlord purposefully clear his throat.

'I think we are being told to behave, come on John, we must show some decorum.' she said linking his arm and escorting him to the bar. 'You sit there, landlord, a beer please.'

'Don't fuss me, I'm alright.' said John sitting down on one of the bar-stools.

'Are you ok, they forced me to run, said the same would happen to me, I'm sorry John ... I'm so sorry.' she said leaning in, tears briefly appearing in her eyes.

'Emily don't be so bloody silly, I warned you the kind of world that I am from if anything ever happens to me you are to run, you understand me run as fast and as far as you can.'

The landlord placed a beer on the bar walked back to serve another patron.

John picked up his beer and enjoyed the first gulp immensely.

'Well come on how are you? What happened?'

John explained the events of the last week leaving nothing out. She listened intently, engrossed and horrified as the tale unfolded.

'Yet you still came here, to meet me, you braved it all again just to try and find me?'

John flushed red. 'You're worth it.'

Emily leant forward and kissed him.

'So what now John? Am I in danger as well?'

John shifted uncomfortably on his stool. 'I have been assured that you're not, to be fair the doctor does usually keep his word, if he says you're going to die, you die.'

'Has he said you are going to die?' said Emily grabbing his hands.

'No that is the strangest thing for some reason he is toying with me. Why is he leaving you out of it? Why did help nurse me back to health? How did they know where I would be? And therefore how did they know about you?'

John gulped down his beer and politely asked the landlord for another one.

I must have had a tail and a very good one. The gates at the factory are more explainable in hindsight, they know I am not one to shy away from a fight, but it does not explain what difference the day makes though.'

'Stop thinking about it, just relax and enjoy my company for now. I know we haven't known each other long but I want you to know that I am very fond of you.'

'And I am of you.'

As they chatted and the hours flew by they did not notice anyone else in the pub, despite John's heightened sense of danger that was now permanently switched on, he got lost in the words of an enchanting goddess that had pulled him into her world. Outside John's mind switched onto full alert, he reached for his gun, but the streets were empty.

'Where do you live Emily?'

'Kensington.'

'You need to get a hansom right now; there'll be one on the next street.'

'I am not afraid of them brutes. I have faced up to plenty of scary men before I can assure you.' Emily said standing there with her hands on her hips.

John stood there bewildered not sure of what to say.

'Besides, I have my umbrella.' she said releasing a smile.

'Oh, of course that will frighten them off. Come on.' said John chuckling but gently pulling her across the road. John paused when they got to the corner of the next road, he drew out his gun but no one was there.

John heard a hansom clopping its way through the quiet night time streets, he waved it down and helped Emily into the cab.

She quickly kissed him and slipped him a piece of paper.

'That is my address, come and visit me on Saturday afternoon at five, I shall make us dinner, if you do not come I will meet you at our usual place at 8 o'clock on Sunday, oh, and please be careful John.' she seductively blew him a kiss.

    John, turning bright red as usual, gave a shallow nod. He pulled out some money and slipped it to the driver; it was more than double the fare.

    'Make sure she gets home safe and when I say safe I mean you are not to leave until she is in the house with the door shut behind her.'

    The driver with his well groomed hair grunted a response and disappeared into the night.

    John returned to the spot where he was attacked, his gun loaded and cocked in his pocket. There was no point in hiding if there was a trap he might as well spring it. Nothing, not even a stranger in a doorway. He walked home uneasy, expecting something sinister to leap out of every shadow, he circled his own street several times checking back alleyways and gardens.

    Once inside he checked every corner of the house, even inside cupboards, behind and under furniture. Nothing was disturbed whatsoever, not a spoon, a picture or chair out of place.

    The daylight seeped through the half drawn curtains John got up and immediately felt thankful that he had gone straight to bed. As he came down the bottom of the stairs, something caught his eye. He looked back into the hall there was a poster nailed on the inside of his door. It read:

Today John 7pm

    John ran to the front door, it was locked fast from the inside, he unlocked it and walked out into the street. One of his elderly neighbours waved a paper at him and trundled back into his house. No one else was there. He ran back in, ripped the note off the door, went to his nearest hiding hole and pulled out another gun. He cursed himself for coming downstairs unarmed. After a complete search, John was baffled at how they managed to enter and put up the poster without waking him.

As he dressed John felt more relaxed, come tomorrow, he would either have a plan on what he was going to do or he would be dead.

The darkness of a winter night had truly enveloped the land by the time it came for John to leave the house for his rendezvous. He armed himself as much as he could; if he was to die he would do it fighting.

He put on many layers including a waistcoat with extra pockets sewn in and a huge thick over coat that had been likewise adapted to hold and conceal extra weaponry. There was no point in being scared, he mustered up every angry thought he could, he imagined Emily being tortured and murdered. As he walked his fists clenched tighter.

He walked into the factory courtyard, there were ugly weather beaten men everywhere, most he knew but there were plenty of new faces as well, the dreaded doctor had been busy. Craig stepped out from the open doors as he did John heard the huge gates close behind him.

'Glad you came John you made the right choice.'

'Did you enjoy yourself the other night my old friend? What's the matter can't face Queensbury rules?'

'That wasn't personal John and you know it, I had to carry out orders just like you did with Jake all those years ago.'

John recalled the incident vividly, just after he had joined the medics one of his friends had disobeyed orders twice and John was instructed to mete out the punishment. He had beaten his friend to a pulp. The memory was as fresh as a cut from his razor that morning.

Craig wearing his usual brown flat cap searched him thoroughly and discovered nearly every hidden blade, baton and gun, but they did not discover the hidden Dillinger on his wrist. John wondered if Craig had missed it on purpose.

John looked around, some familiar faces nodded, others turned away in disgust, he looked for the barrow boy, the runt of the litter that they always made fun of but he was not there. With more than five guns trained in his back, John was frog-marched through the warehouse into a large room right at the back. John had never been into this room but he knew of its existence. It was strictly off limits. He walked in and saw a line of heavyset men standing in front of a desk. He looked to the right and saw Emily sitting on a chair in the corner of the room with two men pointing their guns straight at her. John immediately rushed forward but as he did five guns behind him and the two aimed at the Emily all cocked simultaneously.

John's face screwed up, *'you said you would leave her out of this, where are you? Show yourself coward.'*

The line of men separated revealing the small barrow boy sitting at a desk. The term boy was used to describe him but really he was a man, small in height, rather stocky and constantly ridiculed as the stupid one, but was no one was allowed to lay a hand on him. Yet, if any outsider even smirked at him they would feel the brute force of the Medics.

John stood there with his mouth open like a basking shark feeding on plankton.

'The barrow boy! How could it be you? The doctor, the brains behind the whole operation has been walking amongst us the whole time.' John thought back to all the times that the barrow boy had passed on messages, commands and instructions. The way he was able to pass unnoticed, even in the most confidential meetings, no one would think twice about the barrow boy passing through or even interrupting and joining in.

'Confound you Andy, you're a genius.' John pulled out a cigarette, lit it and threw the dead match onto the desk whilst a plume of smoke erupted from his mouth. 'You are to be congratulated, you have beaten me at every turn, I just wanted to say that before you execute me.'

One of the henchman walked up to John and punched him straight in the face. John's cigarette flew out of his mouth and his head turned but he did not sway, he was a tough man. John brought up his mighty fist up to punch him back but stopped halfway remembering his situation.

'Who said you could speak? In fact who said you could smoke?' the henchman with thick eyebrows and a mop of black hair stared at John.

A split second and the expression in his eyes had changed to shock and horror. John felt the sensation of water being flicked on to his face. The henchman was falling and John saw the penny sized hole in his forehead and realised the back of his perpetrators brains had just been blown all over the wall.

John turned to see where the shot had come from and saw the gun still smoking. He followed the gun up the hand, up the arm, up the shoulders and finally to the face. Never had he seen a face so contorted with malice and eternal rage, scrunched up as tight as it could be and as red as the crimson sun.

'I told you not to hurt him.' said Emily in a tone so gravelled with anger she sounded like a wild animal attempting to talk.

John gasped. Emily was still holding the gun pointing at where the man's head once was and her arm was still shaking with uncontrollable rage. Suddenly Emily's arm moved in one swift action and John heard the gun cock. Following the line of the barrel John quickly determined that she was aiming at another of the henchman.

'No, please, I had no knowledge he was going to do it, I swear it, he stepped out and punched him before I could protest.'

Her was hand still shaking, she looked at him, '*Get out of my sight.*'

The man marched out of the room without looking back. John was still flabbergasted.

'Emily, *you work for the Doctor?*'

The barrow boy burst out laughing but quickly controlled himself. Everyone else stood silent.

Emily finally lowered the gun and approached John walking as demurely as she had when they first met. The room remained silent and her still walk was almost invisible.

She put her hands on his cheeks and looked at him:

'John, *I am the Doctor, the Dreaded Doctor.*'

John looked around the room realising that everyone was waiting on her command, that is why they were not speaking, all this time, it was Emily.

'But you can't be you're a ...'

Emily put her hands on her hips and raised her petite eyebrows. '*A woman?*' she said finishing John's sentence. 'My father was one of the best surgeons in the land, all I had to do was tie my hair, dress like a man and I was trained to be a doctor. I carried on this subterfuge after I had trained but decided that my skills were more entrepreneurial.'

John could not help but snigger.

'Some of my father's friends saw through our skulduggery but no one had anything to gain by betraying us. I have been in love with you for a while but I had to test your mettle, I am sorry darling but it was me that had you beaten so badly. I had to know whether you would still look for me afterwards, if I was worth fighting for and you walked straight to your own death like a real man. Had you failed me I do not know what I would have done as I swore an oath to myself that I would never kill you.

For your information every one of your old gang wanted you killed with the exception of Craig who fought quite admirably, given the circumstances, to protect you. If he were not so certain of his own death, I am quite sure, he would have fought by your side, but you can deal with all that later and however you see fit.

John was still in shock but tried to not to show it. 'You're telling me that I have fallen in love with the most cunning and powerful criminal mastermind ever known to mankind?'

She leant forward and kissed him softly on the lips. 'It is what it is.' she replied.

The Cats of Kensington Mews

'Tell me sir, are you new to Kensington?' asked he.
'Yes, it is a quaint place befitting of both ladies and gentlemen, everything one could ask for.' replied I not sure how to take the boldness of my new friend.

The man laughed a knowing laugh and said 'Beware the Cats of Kensington Mews.'

His retort startled me, and I wondered whether he was a lunatic. I had heard that there was an asylum a couple of miles down the road.

'What on earth do you mean my dear fellow?'
'This is no usual borough of London you know.'
'Pray continue.' I gestured salivating with curiosity.
'You understand that we are right by Kensington palace which is occupied by Queen Victoria herself.'
'Why sir I am a monarchist to the last. I love Queen Victoria as every good Englishman should.'

I remember the man beaming me a huge smile upon hearing this remark. His reaction put me at ease; if he was a madman - he was not a sinister one.

'That is music to my ears. You see us fellow residents are all patriots you know, we love the Queen and we love our country.'

'Absolutely.' I chipped in.

'Yes, but the thing you do not understand is that this neighbourhood is kind of ... well ... magical I suppose.'

'In what way?' I enquired trying not to seem desperate for information.

'As one might imagine the Royal family always need protecting. I tell you we are not the only residents who are sworn to do so. The cats around here protect both the community and the royal family. Remarkably efficient they are too, and much better than we can do.'

I choked upon my ale and wrestled with the idea of remonstrating with the man. I decided upon a half mock.

'Don't be so absurd. How can cats protect the neighbourhood or the queen? Do they walk around like Bobbies with hats and truncheons, blowing their whistles?

I recall the man burst out into raucous laughter which I found to be most irksome given the circumstances. As if making a fool of me was not enough he had to compound it by laughing in my face. Seeing the vexation growing upon me he quickly continued his discourse.

'You misunderstand me sir; these are not normal cats. It is rumoured that when George III was on the throne, the king came to the aid of a small island during an uprising somewhere in the tropics. This tiny island had no way to repay the king so they bestowed upon him two large cats.

They were not tiger, lion, cheetah or even lynx. The king was warned that they were mythical creatures and just like you the king scoffed at this notion ...'

I would have blushed at this point were it not for the absurdity of the story.

'... that was until he saw them. The cats are the size of a small horse and have two tails with a poodle-like ball of fluff at the end of each one. They have big wide mouths with a long almost dog-like tongue, big round eyes, and large cat-like ears that have outer layers so it appears like there is an ear in an ear in an ear, if you follow my path. Despite their size, they appear quite docile and I am reluctant to confess rather cute.'

I remember thinking how impressed I was with his imagination.

'That is ...' he continued 'until they get angry. Their huge dopey mouths fill with vicious long pointed teeth. Claws akin to carving knives burst forth from their feet, their eyes become narrow yellow slits and the fluffy ball of fur at the end of each tail becomes a solid mace of razor sharp spikes. Then they literally tear you to shreds. You remember me saying they are mythical?'

'I recall.' answered I nonchalantly. I was too engrossed in the tale to care about my response indicating my utter disbelief.

'Well, they cannot be seen by everyone ...'

I remember laughing out loud at how convenient this new development was. I had happened upon a charlatan there could be no doubt. I rather enjoyed being the laughing party at that stage.

'Oh how so?' I enquired attempting not to laugh directly in the man's face.

'Well they are mythical you see and one cannot prescribe with precision the physics of a mythical creature can one?'

'In that regard, you must stand correct.' ventured I, feeling safe in the fact that mythical creatures do not exist hence their very description.

'So who *can* they be seen by?' I asked with more than a sprinkling of sarcasm.

'They reveal themselves only to whom they wish.'

The sincerity in his voice said he was scolding me with the answer rather than adding another layer to the fairytale.

'Usually residents of Kensington and the Royal Family of course.' continued he.

'*Laugh in his face or continue the charade?*' scratching my head I chose the latter. 'Anything else I should be aware of?'

'Yes, there is. They can pass through walls and solid objects.'

I spat a mouthful of beer back into my glass and guffawed inconceivably loud. It was too much, and I found myself in a fit of laughter.

'I tell you now my good sir.' said he in a rather forceful voice, 'a would-be burglar tried to flee from one of the cats into another home. The surprise he must have had when it leapt straight from the street into the parlour and ripped him to shreds.'

Laughter took hold of me again, but in the depths of my merriment I was starting to like him and wondered whether he could always provide me with such entertainment. 'Forgive me it is apparent that the beer has more of a hold on me than I had realised.' said I.

'You think I am having a jape with you my good sir. I am not. Of that I assure you. You shall see with time; if you stay the course that is. The man laughed heartily and twiddled his thick brown moustache. I could not help but wonder whether the laugh was again supposed to be at my expense.

'Let us be clear you do have jape with me, but it has been amusing. You would make a great author.' said I, asserting my dominance over his tomfoolery.

I was about to blurt out some distractive remark when he put his hand on my shoulder and said. 'I shall leave you in peace now my good fellow. You can stumble upon me most weekends in this very public house, I pray that you do. My name is Edmond Biggleswade by the way.' said he.

'And I am Richard Baldock.' replied I firmly shaking his hand.

Edmond put on his hat, tipped it at me and bade me goodnight.

After a particularly ghastly ride home on the underground train where I was choked and blinded by acrid smoke, and my bones were rattled so hard I feared that they would break, I found myself pondering Edmond's story. Lunacy maybe, but perhaps it was this that made the prospect of moving to the area more exciting. Upon hearing my interlocutor's tale the decision became certain. After many an enquiry, I found the perfect abode and it will come as no surprise to hear that it was in a mews.

I rapidly forgot my bizarre encounter and became comfortable in my new home and enamoured with my surroundings. Magnificent white houses guarded the kind streets like loyal terriers. Cosy cobbled hideaways invited you forth with ambient lighting. Gentlemen with top hats and cane commanded the pavement. Even trees seem to grow and discard their foliage with an unknown dignity. 'This is indeed royal territory' I remember thinking to myself.

I started becoming a regular down the very public house that I had stumbled upon and first met Edmond in. Yet I had not one sighting of him since the move. I saw plenty of normal cats of course; they stirred my memory somewhat which was displayed via a rather shallow grin.

It was on a rather plain and ordinary Tuesday morning that the subject was once again forced upon me by a neighbour as I strolled down the cobbles. She was a handsome, spritely young woman with lovely brown hair, who I must confess had rather taken my fancy. I had never spoken a word to her hitherto, just gestured politely with my hat, during my general goings about. Upon this particular day, she marched upon me like a fox to a rabbit and placed her hand on my arm. Since we had never been formally introduced I found it rather familiar.

'Have you seen one yet?' she asked.

'Seen what?' I responded.

'You know what I mean?'

'Actually, I do not madam.'

This was true; I found myself quite bewildered.

'The Cats of Kensington Mews. I know you know what I am talking about and you *are* a resident now.'

She stood there staring at me, her brown eyes open wide and standing firm in their challenge.

'I have seen plenty of cats about these parts. You own one yourself do you not?'

'Oh come sir, we both know perfectly well what I'm talking about.'

Her boldness and temerity startled me. As if I was a naughty schoolboy standing in front of the headmaster I blubbed my confession.

'No, I haven't madam, I'm not sure I believe in such fairy tales, if you'll excuse my abruptness.'

She responded to that remark with a loud laugh that to me seemed not too distant from the one that Edmond gave in the pub. She took her gloved hand off my arm and said, 'You will sir I am sure of it and my name is Emily not Madam.'

For an unknown reason I felt embarrassed. 'Apologies, my name is Richard.' said I.

Abruptly she walked away chuckling to herself.

I felt I was the only one who did not know something. It was then that I wondered whether it was some sort of communal conspiracy. My cousin had recently relayed a story to me that in the factories by the docks a newcomer had to pass through several initiating japes before they were accepted.

That Friday night after a particularly tiresome week I headed on down to the public house and allowed myself to get rather inebriated. After talking to, and perhaps bothering, most of the patrons I stumbled out into the night. I stopped and stood there in a state of mumchance. For what I had seen as I rounded the corner was a large cat-like creature reminiscent of a tiger in size. It disappeared *into* a wall with its two bobble tipped tails following behind it.

After what might have been seconds or minutes I wended my way home. The next day I awoke with the memory sticking to me like a nightmare that forces one out of the security of their beds to seek a medicinal cup of tea.

Had I really seen what I thought I had seen? Could the fabled Cats of Kensington Mews really exist? Emotionally stirred, my mind was whirring like a chronometer, our happily adopted beverage calmed my nerves and regained my composure. Of course I had been mistaken, people were filling my mind with ridiculous ideas. Convinced I had allowed myself to see what other people thought I should rather than what I actually did, I set about my usual business.

Again my reader let us travel together in time; it was some two weeks later. A dry and cold Friday and as usual in the evening I was to be found in the pub that I had first discovered. I must confess to being somewhat guilty where inebriation is concerned, but despite all the patrons leaving I was still of my own mind. Myself and the landlord having now become friends had a quiet whisky together. Then I bade him farewell.

Upon leaving the premises I fell into a fine state. The perfect balance between inebriation and coherence. As I Strolled by the wall, which had an opening into another mews, I heard muffled voices coming from the other side. As I listened I realised that they were sotto voce.

'I'm telling you Fred, no one knows us around here.'

'Yeah alright then me old mucker lets find someone to tumble with.'

My senses kicked into high gear and I was filled with the sobering power of adrenaline. These recidivists were obviously up to no good, and I was right near my own front door. It would not take me long to reach it. Fast, silent strides were what was required. As soon as I was in my home I would lock the door and not open it until morning.

'Why hallo there sir.' came the gruff voice. 'Might I trouble you for the time?'

'*Confound it.*' I cursed to myself. Now I was cornered. If I opened my door they would be on me, luckily it was not obvious where I was heading to, so the protection of my worldly goods became my bigger concern.

'Good evening kind sir, alas I left my pocket watch at home but allow me to bid you a merry evening.' I said tipping my hat toward them.

They had marched themselves upon me before I had even finished the sentence and to plead innocence and general bemusement was all I could do. One of the ruffians with grey-flecked stubble and a flat grey cap came close up to my face as if to announce his halitosis.

'You wouldn't be a fibber by any chance would you? You see me and my friend here, have heard that you all carry one around these ere parts.'

I fluttered my eyelids and shook my head as if I was bewildered by the question. 'As I previously mentioned on a normal occasion I do, but tonight I forgot I am not sure how I can be of any assistance.'

The other ruffian stepped forward. He was clean shaven with a heavily scarred face and bad teeth. 'You can be of assistance by emptying your pockets.'

My mouth dropped open and my heart stammered like a madman smashing keys on a piano, the blood drained from my face.

'Acting scared won't save you matey.' the one with cap hissed.

I just stood there transfixed in a state of mumchance.

'Did you hear us?' the other one snapped.

'Yes.' I muttered, dismissing him as if I were talking to a waiter. All I could do was stare at the tiger sized cat, with a long droopy tongue, large ears, two bobbled tails and round eyes that stood there looking at me. It looked dopey and friendly as if it were my own cat who wanted to come and sit on my knee. It was so big I was afraid to look away.

Finally, it dawned on the men that it was not them who had my attention and they turned to see what had me so mesmerised. They turned around and as soon as they did it transformed. The fluffy balls of wool on its tail turned to vicious spikes, its eyes changed from being round to being slits, it's long dopey tongue retracted and its mouth filled with large almost shark-like teeth. Huge razor-sharp claws burst forth from its massive furry paws.

The men were more shaken than I. The three of us stood there like statues.

'R ... r ... run.' the smaller man stammered. As soon as they turned to run the mythical feline charged. With nothing but terror running through my veins I flinched and coiled up as if I should once again be in my mother's arms. The cat ran past me. Having never witnessed a cheetah I cannot be certain just how fast they can run, but I am confident this cat would have beat it.

In seconds it was on the larger man and tore him asunder. The shorter one stopped dead in his tracks as another of the cats appeared in the entrance to the mews. He backed himself against a wall.

'I'm sorry we didn't mean any trouble, *I'm sorry.*' he now almost squealed as he sighted his dismembered friend laying on the floor. He saw the cat who had shredded his accomplice skulking purposefully toward him. It seemed that the other cat was just keeping him from escape.

'*No, please.*' I heard the poor devil yelp as he literally fell to pieces. As the man lay in a pile of unrecognisable parts the giant cat, now returning to its former self, gave me an adoring look as if a cat had just dropped a dead sparrow on your doorstep. In an automated response not quite my own I tipped my hat at it. Remarkably with not one bit of blood upon it, the cat looked at me and then darted through the side of a wall.

I looked at the mews entrance. The other cat had disappeared as well. With too much to process I bolted into my house and locked the door fast. I retired to bed trying to convince myself that it was all but a drunken illusion.

The next morning it was as if nothing had ever happened, but the neighbourhood had changed. Everybody chuckled knowingly in my direction and I began seeing the cats on a daily basis. On one particular sunny morning, one came bounding out of the side of a house and stood in front of me. Hitherto, I had always made good my escape but this time I stood my ground. It walked slowly toward me, jumped up and placed its huge paws on my shoulders. It was so heavy it nearly brought me crashing to the ground. The huge cat licked my face and started making a fuss of me. I confess never had I had such an excitable reaction since I was young and I will gladly confess that I smiled with glee. And who should walk past but none other than Emily who had quizzed me so determinedly.

'Oh, quite right you are. I see you do not believe in fairy tales at all do you?' said she laughing heartily.

And that my dear reader brings us to the end of my anecdote. Guilt is the only thing I feel now as I cannot seem to place a fitting way to end my tale. Should not every good story sign off with some compelling conclusion? What words of wisdom could I possibly bestow upon you?

Oh, my dear reader, of course, I have something to say, something to leave you with, something for you to take home. What is it you ask?

Why it is this: Beware the Cats of Kensington Mews!

Swing II

    'I was of a more sprightful age when I bore witness to a most remarkable event.'
    'In your youth sir?'
    'A young man perhaps in my early twenties as I recall.' A plume of smoke covered the man's face briefly as his pipe burst to life like a dormant volcano. 'Full maturation may still have evaded me; on that we might agree.' the man said chuckling out thick smoke from between his teeth.
    'Maturation evades most for some time Thomas, our offspring can testify to that.'
    Thomas sat there musing over the comment with a smile. He was a man of both medium height and stature, sporting a blue velvet waistcoat and black suit. The dark brown hair was starting to grey and age began to haunt his countenance.
    'In an attempt to avoid the humdrum of the endless back lanes and alleys in the big smoke we would often attempt to explore as much of London as we could. One day we stumbled upon a quarry and spent endless hours using it as our personal playground. It was this quarry that had returned to our memories and thusly a re-visit was proposed.'

'Yes, I know that claustrophobic feeling all too well. Unless you have lived it one can never understand the exasperation that such a childhood can bring. It astounds me that I have now chosen to remain in these conditions by still living in our fine capital.'

Thomas pulled the pipe out of his mouth and guffawed 'Ha, I suspect you have improved your lot somewhat sir. Don't you?'

'Yes I suppose I have Thomas.' a brief snigger escaped, Howard's eyes twinkled with mischief.

Thomas examined him studiously. Howard was of slight obesity with prematurely grey hair and an ill-fitting expensive brown suit.

'I know your devilry Howard you would have jape with me.'

'Indeed I would old man. Indeed I would. Pray, continue.' Howard said chuckling away to himself.

As I recall the weather was fair that day, warm and inviting, we had no requirement for our outer coats, we all wore shirts and waistcoats I believe.

'Confound you, why have you brought a ball with you Victor?'

'In order to play some football a man must keep in shape you know.'

'That may be, but we are visiting a quarry.'

'Thomas your vexations are too much, are we still not in our youth, in our prime as it were. What harm can it do?'

'Frank, I am merely surprised is all.'

'You merely cannot play football is the more likely outcome.'

'Oh ha, bloody ha John. We shall see eh?'

'That we will, now cheer up the quarry approaches.'

'Yes, come on Thomas.' said Victor playfully shoulder barging him.

Victor was taller than Thomas and lean.

John kicked the pigskin ball up in the air and running in front of them all caught it again with his foot. He was the largest of the men with large broad shoulders; he was also the tallest being slightly taller than Victor.

It was Frank who was the first to reminisce about the days they used to visit this place as children. He ran to the edge of the pit and stood there with his hands on his hips. He was the shortest of the men; he was also slightly rotund but not enough to hinder him from being good at football.

'Many a glorious day we spent here, eh boys?'

'That we did.' I agreed.

Frank fell forward on the edge of the cliff but was abruptly pulled back just in time. 'Saved you from death again.' laughed Victor.

'*You swine,*' yelled Frank throwing his hat at victor and running after him.

'Why nothing has changed at all.' said John flicking the ball up with his foot and heading it over to me.

I fancied it had been a few years since a football had greeted my foot as I recall the reunion was not an unpleasant one. I remember repeatedly kicking it up with one foot, smiling like I was a twelve-year-old boy again.

'Frank calm down and have this.' I said passing him the ball.

He turned and kicked it to John. It was then that I noticed Victor who had been running from Frank had disappeared from view. You must understand that the quarry had changed greatly since our day. It was now vast, with new pits plummeting ever deeper, creating caves, alcoves and caverns which now littered the place.

Victor suddenly reappeared, 'Come hither, quick, you will never guess what I have discovered.'

We all looked at each other and briefly considered just carrying on playing football so we might revel in

Victor's chagrin. Curiosity is a powerful thing though and we all headed over to investigate our friend's discovery.

As we rounded the carved out wall of rock, Victor exclaimed '*Ta-da.*' as if he was some magician in a carnival. It was the largest cavern we had ever seen; its huge grey mouth open like a giant whale ready to swallow us whole.

'It is a cavern.' said I.

'Your observational skills are quite remarkable. Has anyone ever informed you of that?' said Victor with his hands on his hips and a wry smile on his face.

John and Frank laughed vigorously.

'I meant why the excitement?' Replied I hotly.

'Come in and see for yourself.'

We followed Victor into the cave. It was indeed huge and the inside dwarfed the apparently large entrance. Fissures let daylight through at various points lighting up the whole area as if it were some purpose-built arena. A majority of the ground was flat rock and smooth, but there was a large section to the left that consisted of loose rock and shingle.

'Well Victor, it is an impressive cavern that I grant you.' said John with his foot standing on the ball.

'John is right but I do fancy a game chaps if you are up for it?' added frank looking back outside.

'Look that is what I meant to show you, we have our own arena, as long as we do not play near the entrance we can kick it as hard as we like and without fear of it going over the edge of the quarry. I assure you I for one am not going to get it if it does.'

'That is a fair point.' said I.

'And look,' said John pointing toward the back of the cave, 'we can use that alcove as a goal.'

'Pass the ball then John.'

I remember John hoofing the ball far across the cavern and us all laughing about it. '*Goal.*' screamed John as it rolled into the alcove that he had proposed as a goal.

We started playing football when Frank rather unexpectedly kicked the ball far across the cavern into the loose shingle. He ran over to retrieve it. We stood there impatiently waiting for him to return or better yet kick the ball back to us so we could continue unabated.

Frank whose face was normally beetroot in colour looked at us with such an ashen pallor that I swear he was going to drop dead right there and then. His mouth was agape as he stared at us in a state of mumchance.

'What the devil is wrong with you?' I shouted.

'What hinders you man? Kick the blasted ball back.' snapped Victor.

'*Ca ... com ... can't ... come quickly my friends, quickly, a sight so ghastly has befallen me.*'

'Frank, have you been at the opium or something; we are losing patience.'

'*Look,*' he screamed '*Look what is by the ball, just come here and inspect for yourselves.*'

With a murmur of tuts and grunts, we went over to see what had our friend in such a wretched state.

Upon catching up with him we also fell into a state of mumchance. I remember it being John who was the first to pass any verbal exclamation.

'*It is a hand. That is a human hand.*' he shrieked with a tremble in his voice.

There sticking out of the stones was a grubby looking human hand that looked like it had been embalmed in ash. Our eyes rapidly inspected the scene thoroughly to see if we could see a nose or some other feature protruding through the stones. There was nothing.

'Suppose it is just a hand and nothing else.' ventured I.

'You mean we stumbled upon some murderous skullduggery?' said Victor.

'I … I … rather fancy that it has to be murder, what rational explanation can there be for leaving a hand or a body buried under a pile of rocks?' said Frank with the slightest shade of colour returning to his face.

'Perhaps the hand is severed, this is a working quarry, we are on the Sabbath remember? Perhaps some fellow lost his hand the week before and in a hurry to get to the hospital forgot to collect it.' said John rubbing his face.

'We have no choice gentleman we must investigate further. If there is a body we must report it and get this ghastly event off our hands.'

'Well who is going to do it?' said Victor.

'I'm not, you can count on that.' replied Frank.

'Confound you all, we are men now, I'll do it.'

I pulled a couple of large smooth stones from the hand and as I did the rocks all started to slide. Never will I forget it as long as I live, the stones rolling like marbles, it was no landslide we were on flat land. No, it was something rising out of the stones.

It seems almost humorous to me now, the faces of us four men as a corpse started rising from the ground. We all recoiled a few steps gasping with horror. The man sat upright. His complexion was that of Franks a little while previous, but his face was gaunt and his eyes were sunken with a huge thin nose and thinning grey hair. Judging by the length of his torso he was a very tall man, much taller than one would normally expect.

We stood there agog as this spectre sat upright as if he was some kind of machine. His eyes were closed. There was no sign of breathing, no chest movements, his clothes were grubby and torn. He wore a tattered waistcoat over a ripped white shirt which was now a lead grey.

We watched with intense horror each one in our own trance of petrification and amazement. His eyes opened, and I heard John exclaim a small noise of shock daring not to believe what he was seeing. The head turned towards me, the stillness of the creepy grey face unnerved me, how I did not flee in a panic I shall never know.

'I am no apparition, why do you assume so easily?'

'*Good God he's alive.*' exclaimed Victor excitedly.

'Confound your imbecilic ways man, what are you doing buried in the rubble?'

'I was working in the quarry when I had an accident. The fools thought I was dead and buried me. Damn and blast them they could have rushed me to the sawbones, but the scoundrels just buried me.'

Frank pulled out a canteen. 'Here you better have a drink.'

'Much appreciated sir,' he said doffing a hat that wasn't there. His long bony fingers reached for the canteen and drank from it as if it was the first drink he ever had.

'You better finish that my good man.' said Frank genially.

The stranger ignored him continuing unabated until the beverage was finished.

'Why you have laid there all this time is what puzzles me.' said I

'The truth is I am a somewhat ornery fellow and would say more despised than disliked. The accident I had was being hit on the back of the head. The casual way that they buried me laughing suggested to me that this might not have been an accident.' said the man wiping his mouth and leaving a clean spot in the process.

'I was right in diagnosing nefarious skullduggery then.' said Victor.

'Indeed you were.' said the man.

'How did you hear them if you were unconscious?' asked John.

'I was not out for that long. I feared for my life but I have had much experience and have adapted to survive. I knew I must stay buried in case they came back to check, and besides that, this is my home and I wanted to ensure that they would not return.'

'Your home? Talk sense man this is a quarry.' said I, becoming rather annoyed at such a stupid statement.

'I have worked it most of my life even when you were all youngsters.'

'Yes, but it is not your home.' said Frank.

'Let us help the man up.' said Victor.

'There is no need,' said the man rising as if he had buried himself. The stones and pebbles rolled seamlessly from him, and he was so tall that he towered over John. 'I assure you this is my home.'

'Come we must get you a doctor.' Victor said going to touch his arm but then thinking better of it.

'Nonsense, that drink has rehydrated me enough. I only ask that you never tell a soul about my existence. About what happened here lest misfortune and calamity come to visit me once again.'

'We swear as gentlemen of Old London Town never shall we repeat the events of today.'

'Well not for twenty years at least.' the man replied flashing us a warm smile.

I remember it being the first time that we saw any humanness to the man, up until that point he had been monotone, nonchalant in his approach. It was also as I recall the first time I noticed he was wearing suit trousers and indeed shoes.

'I am grateful for your assistance but I have one more thing to ask.'

'What is that Sir.' replied John.

'It will appear rude, and I fancy it is rude, but seeing as I was here first …'

'*You want us to leave?*' I enquired.

The man remained silent with an almost puzzled look on his face.

We all looked at each other mildly embarrassed. The peculiarity of the situation left us no recourse but to agree or get involved in some egregious debate which was wholly unsuitable.

Frank collected the ball.

'Good luck old fellow.' I offered.

'Thank you gentleman.' he said in a stoical voice.

We all walked out of the cave and journeyed back to London discussing the strange affair for the entire journey.

'I tell you Howard nary has there been a stranger tale.'

Howard leant forward finally putting his glass back on the table. 'Yes, it is rather odd.' replied he.

'You know what is strange, I believe there was no such attempted murder. It was all a ruse.'

'You mean he put himself under them stones?'

'Possibly - I don't know, but looking back I am sure he was just wanted rid of us and that he was in no danger. Certainly not from a phantom work party in any case.'

'Was that the last time you saw him?'

'No, it wasn't. Upon retiring to my bed that night I found myself restless, unable to sleep and when I did the man from the quarry haunted me. I saw his face whenever I closed my eyes, he stalked my dreams, I would wake up in the night dripping with cold perspiration, full of anxiety at the strange encounter, what had become of this man? Had we done the right thing? Had we not left him to die?

Perhaps he was ill and could not care for himself. Perhaps there really were killers after him and we had abandoned him like cowards. This all became too much and by the third day I was seeing his face in the daytime. Every time I pulled back the parlour curtains I would expect to see his face staring back at me. Finally, I could take it no more and I wandered alone to the quarry.

I remember the day, to me the sun had a particular poignancy. It was late in the afternoon when I arrived and the sky was bright red. I crept up to the perimeter. Upon seeing nothing of interest I crept forward and gaining confidence I walked to the edge of the quarry. What I saw has haunted me ever since, yet I cannot explain why.

There was a set of swings as one might see in child's play park or garden but it was slightly larger than usual. There were two swings housed in a typical frame that appeared to be made out of the rock.

The most remarkable thing was that the old man from the quarry was on one of them; swinging back and forth as high as he could go. His legs were stretched out and he leant back to gain full momentum, he was wearing the same dirty clothes with the same waistcoat, but now he had a top hat to go with it. He cackled, laughed and screeched with every swing.

A Hebridian Adventure

Why is it some folk persist in pointless hobbies or pastimes? A symphony of bird and insect filled the air as I was reading a broadsheet article about the newly created Morse code and its messages via electronic telegram. A man came bursting excitedly from the back entrance of my house.

'Hallo James, I have the most excitable tale to tell you.'

'Giles, considering you have been exploring well known chartered waters I find that difficult to believe.'

'Ha!' my friend snorted whilst helping himself to a seat.

'Help yourself to tea *old man*.' I gestured.

He gave me a brief snippet of disgust at this remark for I still looked particularly young. My friend helped himself to a cup of tea from the pot.

'Well come on then man.' said I.

'*I told you, I told you.*' he exclaimed jumping out of his seat.

'*Sit down you confounded lunatic.*' I ejaculated, '*What on earth will the neighbours think?*'

He sat there smiling at me.

'Professor James Bedford, I always told you someone would miss something somewhere and I would find it. Well, at last I have discovered it.'

'Discovered what?' asked I.

'A new island.'

'*A new island!*' repeated I. 'In Great Britain don't be so absurd. These waters have been explored for hundreds of years; why there is not even a barnacle unchartered I imagine.'

My friend had a most serious expression and in sotto voce he said to me, '*That's not all my friend; there is something strange upon it.*'

'Giles, this story grows weirder by the second. Where is this island?'

He lowered his voice even further.

'*The Outer Hebredies.*' I repeated at great volume.

'*Be quiet man. I do not want the whole world to know.*'

It was at this point that my friend's sincerity realised itself upon me. Topping up my teacup I settled in for the story, recognising my change in posture, Giles assumed a similar position.

'As you know I have recently been exploring the Scottish isles. With clusters of islands everywhere I realised there was a higher probability of stumbling across something undiscovered be it a bay or a cave. As you are aware, the weather has been particularly pleasant for the last week or two and after sailing around most of the islands I found myself rather frustrated. Everywhere I went the places were named and people were already occupying them.

In my mind, I assigned it to the continual defeat that an explorer must face. I decided to lay back in my craft and enjoy the congenial sunshine. With the warmth of the sun and the sway of my boat I quickly fell asleep and was soon dreaming of pleasant things. It must have been a rogue wave that awoke me for suddenly my boat was jerked violently.

Snatched from my nirvana I realised was in the open ocean. My skin felt tender I must have slept long in the sun as its damage was already upon me. Panic ensued because adrift the currents could have taken me anywhere. Looking at my pocket watch, I discovered I had been asleep for nearly five hours. As I frantically searched for my compass a green flash crossed my visual spectrum. I halted my search.

The island was different it did not appear to be Hebridian. At first I thought it tropical, the shapes and sizes of the foliage were all at odds with what I know of the Scottish isles. Bewitched I continued to study the approaching anomaly and now relaxed I immediately spotted my compass that had somehow fallen on a coil of rope.

I remember toasting my good fortune with a beer that I had brought with me. Uncorking the bottle with my teeth I spat it out on the deck with the map laid out in front of me. I lifted the compass and nearly choked when I saw where I was. Initially, I had assumed it must be *St Kilda* but the nearest landfall was the *Isle of Lewis* between *Arnol* and *High Borve*.

After double-checking it wasn't the *Flannan Isles* I violently shook the compass and tapped it. The compass remained the same; I had stumbled upon an uncharted island. The closer that I got the more I became certain. It was so remarkably different that had I known about it I would have already explored it thoroughly. Becoming excited I got my wooden rule and started marking the exact route I must have come. I leapt from the boat upon reaching the shore and brazenly walked up the white sandy beach wishing I had brought a flag carrying my family coat of arms or something.

'Hallo there.' I shouted.

To be frank, I expected an answer but it never came. Looking around I noticed there was not one sign of human life. Not a scrap of paper, discarded cigarette or beer bottle, absolutely nothing. Could it be that all the ships that have passed through these waters over the centuries have missed this island by some freakish chance?

With the air still warm and the sun still shining I came toward junglelike scrub; big tall trees and dense woodland stood as if challenging me to enter. Exploration is not for the faint of heart and as it is now my trade I fearlessly stepped forward. Within a minute I heard a mighty thud and a noise that seemed like an entire tree was splitting in half. Rooted to the spot in partial fear I assessed the situation. Another huge thud then another. I felt the ground tremor, then an almighty shriek as if a thousand elephants had been slain all at once.

Loud crashes, cracks, thuds; something orange flashed through the trees. I turned and ran back to my boat swearing to return better prepared.'

'Well? The orange flash what was it old man? A tiger?'

'Hardly,' my friend remembered his tea and drank some after wiping his thin moustache he continued. 'You misunderstand it was big, very big, bigger than a house I tell you.'

'*Bigger than a house don't be so absurd.*' replied I.

'I tell you James it was huge, gargantuan.' said Giles stretching out his arms for dramatic effect.

'Orange you say? It was probably a glimpse of the dying sun flashing through the trees.'

'What with a God awful screech and a terrifying stamp? Besides the sun was still far from setting.'

'Mmm' said I rubbing my chin.

'I saw enough to be certain.'

'To be certain of what?'

'To be certain that there is an adventure to be had!'

'Don't follow old man.' said I lifting up the teacup for some much needed refreshment.

'Are you obtuse? We must go and explore, discover.'

'It might be worth a holiday at some point even if it is to see a thunderous sunset.' said I accidentally releasing a mischievous grin.

'*Confound you James, are you blind man we need to go – now.* This is an undiscovered island with some great mystery upon it ... make haste ... let us explore ... conquer!'

I confess never had I seen my friend so worked up and he had been involved in some successful archaeology previously. A truth started to dawn on me albeit unwanted that indeed my friend was onto something. The strange fauna that he had mentioned and since forgot weighed on me like an anchor in the ocean of truth. Giles was also an ardent botanist it seemed most odd that he could not identify them. Whether it be nothing but some strange plants it could still be a discovery.

'By Jove!' I ejaculated, 'We will set off at once!'

A large smile crossed Giles' face. 'You have yielded to sense Professor James.'

'I told you not to call me that, Giles Lincoln.'

Giles looked at me and chuckled. If you wonder about the reference, I taught a foreign student several years back and he mistakenly thought James was my surname, of course as soon as my friends and compatriots heard it ...'

'Let us fetch Andrew and Gilbert as well.' said Giles

'Yes, but we must take caution Gilbert's quarrelsome daughter has quite a spirit and if she discovers our plans she will be with us.'

'Let us prepare and leave on the morrow.'

'Yes, let's.' remarked I.

Now is the point that, for your sake reader, I shall move the narrative along. Lest to say that after heated words with my wife we all rendezvoused at the station.

There was myself, Giles, Andrew, Gilbert and much to my chagrin Gilbert's daughter Elizabeth. Two younger gentleman also joined us by the name of Dean and Humphrey. They were both academic, keen researchers and even keener explorers. They were as giddy as schoolchildren going on their first summer holiday. It irked me initially but I realised I would be glad of the extra company should we run into trouble. I also reasoned they might assist in keeping that infernal Elizabeth at bay or least in check.

The train journey was long; I know not what we swapped more of – trains or seats. As you can imagine by the time we reached the west coast of Scotland we were more than well acquainted with each other and had resorted to playing card games to alleviate the boredom. The only event in the journey being when Elizabeth had an outburst after losing a hand and stormed out of the carriage only to return fifteen minutes later feigning she had felt unwell.

Early the next day we found ourselves eating in a local pub. So excited was Giles was about his discovery that he had left his boat moored up near Saltcoats and took the train home as it is quicker. We sat around the pub table happily talking and discussing tomorrow's adventure.

'So we shall set off on the morrow.' said I.

'Yes, it is too much to undertake today after the ghastly journey we had getting up here.' said Elizabeth cutting off a sliver of meat and putting it into her mouth.

'That portion is incredibly small Elizabeth it would not do me as a starter.'

'That is probably because you're a pig.' replied Elizabeth with a sharp grin.

Dean rubbed his blonde goatee that like his hair was unkempt. 'Takes one to know one.' he said stuffing an inordinately large piece of meat noisily into his mouth.

Myself and Giles exchanged a conspiratorial look as the ruse was working. The younger men were keeping Elizabeth on her toes and more importantly distracted. Humphrey gauging we were about to get down to business craned his neck in our direction. Despite being the youngest he was the best turned out. A hard confession to make - but every day he was immaculate from his shoes and suit to the parting in his hair.

'If we set off early how long until we arrive?' said Gilbert who was a lot younger than he appeared. His hair having prematurely greyed had betrayed him somewhat. One of the reasons I suspect that he was always clean shaven. Lest anyone think his years were higher than what they were.

'If we are to set off on the morrow let us not waste the day. I suggest that after lunch we prepare the boat and fill it with supplies and the like. Let us have it fully prepared and set off first thing.' said Andrew, his florid cheeks redder than usual as if in competition with his ginger hair.

'Yes a good idea.' said I. 'Gentlemen, I think we have ourselves an organised excursion, is there anything we have overlooked?'

'Do we have boxes and Jars for specimens and artefacts?' asked Humphrey.

'Do you not know me? My boat is laden with such objects.' said Giles

'What about protection?'

'Yes we have protection Dean, several of us have revolvers and there are a couple of rifles hidden on the boat as well.' replied Gilbert.

'We also have knives and machete's.' Andrew added.

'We are in Scotland. At best, all we are likely to find is a long lost, forgotten plant or something.' said I.

'And don't you forget our agreement James.' said Giles finishing my sentence. 'Yes, yes I shall not forget, if we find nothing I shall fund the trip myself. Why if that is the case even the food you are eating shall be reimbursed.' said Giles with a smug grin.

'I was not going to mention it actually.' I retorted with a sheepish smile.

As we sat there I recalled the time that Giles had tried to get me on one of his more exotic adventures. I had declined but seeing the camaraderie between us all I regretted it. I kept this to myself and swallowed it with a spoonful of potato.

We spent the afternoon packing the ship and after many confrontations with Elizabeth who insisted upon rearranging the boat to her fancy succeeded upon finishing. In the evening we found ourselves at a quaint pub on the windswept seafront of *Saltcoats*.

The only factor we had not considered in our careful planning was how accommodating the locals were. The pub was full to the brim of folk wishing to exchange tales, eat heartily and drink merrily. A delicious warm smell of home cooked food, beer and good spirit tempted any passer-by. We were quite the worse for wear by the time we got to bed, being a heavy drinker I awoke in a fairly normal state at a decent hour.

By nine o'clock we had set sail, the sun was warm and the sweet smell of adventure filled our nostrils. Setting off, we drank a few beers to lessen the effects of the night before. We were soon in the open seas. It was gone lunchtime when Giles shrieked excitedly.

'*You see Gentleman there she is - I told you there was an undiscovered island.*' cried Giles.

We all gathered in haste at the front of the boat.

'*By Jove.*' exclaimed I. 'That does not seem like any other island I have seen around our isles.'

Giles was right the island appeared almost tropical, yet somehow not quite. It was as if someone had created a hybrid. Giles left the front of the ship to steer us in.

Andrew was the first ashore. Humphrey was last along with Elizabeth who was helped down with that infernal large leather bag that was not far off being a portmanteau.

'*Why do you need to bring that blasted bag for?*' shouted Gilbert.

'A woman needs her things father, do not be so rude.'

'*You'll slow us up, you stupid child.*'

'I will do no such thing.' she retorted in an insolent manner.

'I shall carry it if need be.' said Humphrey picking it up.

Gilbert snorted his disapproval while the rest of us stood there in an awkward silence. The one thing I have failed to mention was that Elizabeth was very attractive. She had a cute face with a mouse like nose and long blonde hair that always seemed to fall in an evocative manner. Elizabeth had at least opted to wear trousers, which for her, was surprisingly practical.

'It is a bizarre looking island for Scottish waters I will give you that.' said I looking at the foliage in amazement. We hurried up the beach to examine the plants.

'*I don't believe it. Look at this.*' shouted Dean.

'What is it?' enquired Elizabeth.

'*This plant ... it's ... it's extinct!*'

'What are you on about man.' exclaimed Giles marching over. '*Good grief*, you are right Dean, how could I have missed it. This plant was supposedly extinct years ago.'

'What like fifty years - years ago?'

'*Don't be so absurd.*' replied Giles

'*I am not the botanist.*' retorted Humphrey.

'It's prehistoric. Late Cretaceous I think.' said Gilbert.

We all stood there in stunned silence.

'Are you sure old boy?' asked I.

'Certain.' replied Gilbert still looking amazed.

Humphrey and Dean eagerly collected some samples as did Giles who returned to the boat to collect a special jar like container. He dug up a whole plant and carefully placed it in the container complete with roots and earth.

It took time but Giles was immensely pleased to have absolute proof aboard his boat. His triumphant return was already guaranteed. We carefully marched inland, the foliage was thick and unusual yet we did not encounter any giant spiders or insects as one would normally associate with a jungle. It slowly occurred to us that this was still a Scottish isle.

We must have been about thirty minutes into our walk when I heard a shriek from Giles who was leading the advance. I rushed to the front.

'Jupiter be praised look what I have found.' he leant down and picked up the largest feather that I have ever seen. It was taller than he was. He picked it up using two hands and we all marvelled at it like a caveman seeing fire for the first time. The feather was orange like the setting sun with a huge black stripe across it.

'*Confound it, tigers are not that big.*' ejaculated Humphrey.

'Tigers don't have feathers.' remarked Andrew.

'And tigers are not the size of large buildings.' added Giles.

'You mean to tell me that this is from whatever you saw upon first discovering the island?' said I.

'Exactly James.' he replied. 'A great big orange streak the size of a house - what else could it be?'

'A giant chicken perhaps.' cackled Elizabeth.

'You might not say that when you meet it.' replied Gilbert.

Elizabeth placed her large leather bag down ignoring her father's remark. Gilbert maintained his sullen look.

'So what is it some cousin of the cassowary perhaps?' returned I.

'Who knows but it must be what I saw.' replied Giles

A sense of unease passed amongst us and we all grabbed for our weapons.

'Well lest we heed more caution as we go forth.' said Gilbert.

'And more silence.' added Humphrey.

The temperature in the thick Scottish jungle grew pleasant with the leaves and trees protecting them from the hot summer sun.

'It feels weird being in Scotland and not knowing what we are going to run into.'

'Believe me Dean I know that feeling,' replied Giles, 'it was I who-'

A very loud thud brought them to a startling halt.

'What on earth?' said Gilbert.

'I am afraid that is precisely the question.' added I.

Another loud thud.

'*What shall we do?*' shrieked Elizabeth.

Another loud thud.

'We need to find out what we're dealing with.' said Dean

Another loud thud.

'It's coming closer gentleman, we need to make a decision.' said Andrew.

A loud crack as if a large branch or small tree had been brought down.

'We must see what it is.' said Giles.

'If it is that big it is likely to be dangerous.' cried Humphrey.

'That is true even if it is a herbivore it could still be dangerous look at how many people are killed by elephants and hippos.' said Gilbert.

'Whatever it is, it is coming. What shall we do?' said Elizabeth sounding concerned.

'I think we need to observe it before making any rash decisions.' said I.

'You mean hide?' replied Giles.

'Well for now ... yes.' replied I.

'There might be some logic in that there is no need in starting a panic unnecessarily.' said Gilbert.

'I concur.' said Andrew.

After another thunderous crash, a huge orange blur appeared through the trees.

'*Yes, let's hide.*' cried Elizabeth.

We all dived for nearest tree or bush. I glanced around the trunk to get a look at whatever it was that was coming. The creature was enormous it must have been over nine metres tall and it stood on two mighty tree trunk legs with smaller forearms that had terrible long claws at the end of them. Its face had a long snout full of huge razor-sharp teeth and was covered in orange feathers adorned with a black stripe.

Astonished I reached for my hip flask so I might somehow wake up out of the dream. I looked at the others with wondrous terror.

'*It's a Dinosaur!*' I screamed.

'*Dinosaurs don't have feathers.*' yelled Gilbert.

'*Well you try and tell him that.*' said I excitedly pointing at the dinosaur.

'Is ... it a ... T-Rex?' asked Elizabeth nearly too scared to look.

'No, the snout is wrong.' said Dean.

'And the arms.' added Giles.

'I can't believe we have found a dinosaur.' remarked Humphrey stepping out from behind his tree into plain sight.

'Careful old boy.' ventured I.

'*Elizabeth you stay where you are.*' shouted Gilbert.

'*No fear of that Father!*' replied Elizabeth

Slowly and somewhat nervously we all emerged from our hiding places.

'It looks like a giant chicken to me.' said Elizabeth.

'*Get back behind the tree you infernal woman why won't you listen to me?*' screamed Gilbert.

'Father, leave me be.' she pouted.

'I don't know which is the greater discovery, the dinosaur or the fact that it has feathers.' said Andrew.

'It may run deeper than that.' said Giles.

'How so?' ventured I.

'Well, Dinosaur translates as-'

'*Terrible Lizard.*' said Humphrey excitedly finishing Giles' sentence.

'Correct.' replied Giles.

'Not following your path old fellow.' said Andrew doing up his shoelaces.

'What if we have been wrong all along what if instead of lizards they were, in fact more genetically linked to-'

'*Birds.*' shrieked Dean.

'That is a startling thought Giles.' said I.

'That it is James and quite a revolutionary one yet at look at the evidence laid out before our eyes.'

'You don't think a mad scientist is doing experiments of some kind do you?' asked Humphrey.

'That is absurd. These *must be* the very last dinosaurs. Somehow God has blinded mankind to this island until now.' said Gilbert pulling a leaf out of his grey hair.

'We can't go to the science community with that we would be laughed out of London.' cried Andrew.

'No we won't,' replied Giles. 'Not if we have proof.'

'Yes, that sounds excellent.' said Dean.

'We must plan carefully but I agree we will be the toast of the exploratory world. Let us obtain conclusive proof and then announce our findings along with some of our own conclusions.' said I.

'So how do we go about getting this proof?' asked Elizabeth.

'Well we already have a feather.' remarked Andrew.

'Yes and perhaps we can get some plaster casts.' said Humphrey.

'There maybe eggshells we can collect also.' remarked Gilbert.

'Well let us gather the evidence and observe all we can then head home.' said I.

'We need to be *bleedin careful.* I suspect this Dinosaur won't be the friendly sort.' remarked Gilbert glancing at his daughter.

'How do you think it hunts?' asked Elizabeth.

'By smell and sight I imagine.' said Andrew.

The dinosaur snapped its head in their direction and thudded towards them.

'*Confound it, it has seen us.*' cried I.

'Surely not.' replied Giles.

'*Run.*' screamed Humphrey.

We hid behind the trees as the dinosaur came running. The ground shook. I remember motioning to Elizabeth to keep perfectly still. The great beast stopped, lowered its snout and started sniffing at the tree that Gilbert was behind.

Giles motioned to Gilbert not to panic. A few seconds later it withdrew its head and we breathed a sigh of relief; that is until Elizabeth let out a blood-curdling scream that struck terror into all of us.

To this very hour I cannot fathom how it managed to do so, but a second dinosaur appeared out of nowhere and immediately singled out Elizabeth. I pulled out my revolver and started firing. Chaos broke out, those who had guns started firing in every direction. It was only then that we realised we had forgotten to collect the rifles.

We scattered, the dinosaur got distracted and instead of going for Elizabeth it leapt forward and grabbed poor Humphrey as he ran from his tree towards me. I will never forget that crunch as the dinosaur ate him as if he was a handful of nuts.

'The bullets aren't working; their feathers must be too thick.' cried Giles.

'Aim for its head.' yelled Andrew.

For a moment we all regained hiding places. Dean, Giles and Elizabeth were ashen white; the spectre of panic had them possessed.

We watched as the orange and black feathered beasts fought over what was left of Humphrey. I saw Elizabeth vomit. I reloaded my gun and watched Andrew and Giles do the same. Giles motioned for us to retreat as quietly as we could. I held my aim and shot one in the mouth. It seemed to bounce off but had then it held its head up and let out a painful squeal.

The other dinosaur was almost upon us. We stopped, fired some shots at it and then ran. I heard a scream and turned to see that Andrew had been caught. He was still alive in the jaws of the great bird. Blood was spraying everywhere and he was punching at its mouth as hard as he could, screaming in agony. Myself and Giles emptied the rest of our guns into it but not aiming for its head for fear of hitting

Andrew. The bullets seemed to sting the bird enraging it, but there was no sign of injury.

We watched in horror as it dropped Andrew to the floor from a great height. He landed with a thud; blood splashing up as he did so.

The other Dinosaur joined in and for a moment there was a weird stand-off between us all. We stood transfixed in both horror and amazement staring at these magnificent creatures that still had the remains of our friends around their mouths.

In the most bizarre encounter, perhaps in the history of man, we all sensed the standoff was coming to an end. Albeit the giant creatures were feathered I could see their muscles tightening underneath ready for attack. I prepared my mind to fire into its face hopefully between the eyes. My palm grew sweaty, one of the monsters twitched its huge clawed arms, instinctively I brought up my hand. The game was on, both of the dinosaurs stepped forward. Just as the first shot was about to be discharged we heard an almighty voice scream out through the Scottish jungle.

'*Och, what the bloody hell is goin' on ere?*' A giant of a man about six feet seven inches tall stepped out holding the largest fire torch I have ever seen. We all stopped and stared and to our unending astonishment so did the dinosaurs. The man stepped forward holding the mobile bonfire up in the air.

'*Get outta ere you stupid creatures.*' he shouted. The man with his long black curly hair and overgrown beard looked and gazed upon the bloodied corpse of Andrew.

'*Christ, look at what yer done. Look yer stupid bastards.*'

The dinosaurs stood there looking half bewildered, yet half obsequious. The caveman's face flushed red with anger.

'*Get out o' here I tell ya.*' he commanded.

The great beasts just stood there. Suddenly the man charged at them holding the torch up and screaming what sounded to be an ancient Scottish battle cry. The dinosaurs turned on their heels and fled.

'Caveman, thank you for saving us.' said Gilbert beaming a huge smile.

'*I am no caveman you bloody great fool.*' follow me if you want to survive; they won't be frightened for long.'

The man abruptly turned and started walking, his clothes suggested he lived outdoors, they were thick and cumbersome despite it being the height of summer. We all followed in silence not even Elizabeth said a word.

We trudged for over half an hour by my reckoning before we came to a clearing. The bright sunshine hit our eyes which was magnified by the white sand.

We realised this clearing was purposefully made. A huge swathe of jungle had been cleared out and in the middle of it was a large stone cottage. The cottage had been built on the edge of the beach the woodland cut back so that the beach came inland and encompassed the cottage. You could still see tree stumps in the sand.

'You better come inside the lot of yer.' he said as we continued to follow in silence. We entered the cottage and into a huge room that was deliciously cool and had the aroma of old stone. The room had a surprisingly large amount of seating in it. There were numerous chairs as well two really large couches the likes of which I have never seen before.

'Have a seat, I'll put the kettle on and you can explain to me what you English folk are doing trespassing on my island.'

'*Trespassing by Jove.*' ejaculated Giles leaping from his chair. '*What do you mean by that?*'

'I mean this is a private island. What rights have yer bein on it?'

'Now hold on one minute sir, this island is unchartered.' said I.

'Aye and its supposed to be yer English moron. Have yer not seen what happens when you go sticking yer nose in.'

I leapt to my feet in anger and felt my fists clench. Gilbert stood up and grabbed my arm.

'We can see that you are agitated and indeed as well as trespassing on your island we have brought calamity to it. Yet as you yourself point out we have just lost two friends and dear colleagues. We came to your island for adventure and discovery but instead found disaster and misfortune. Please explain to us what this place is so we might understand and try and assuage our grief with scientific understanding. This will put us in better preparation to bury our friends.' said Gilbert sitting back down.

The large man pulled something out of his beard and discarded it to the floor as if he were still outside. 'You won't be burying your friends I'm afraid as you're not going back out there. You'll have to report that they were buried at sea. Since I cannot imprison yer and you would only bring people back ere I will offer you the truth in return for your silence.'

'Steady on old chap, this is the greatest discovery since the Americas.' cried Dean.

'Och, I will not say a word if ye don't promise, this island has been undisturbed for thousands of years. It is not becoming a tourist attraction on my watch.

'I recall the scientist in me came to the fore and I realised how correct his attitude was. What an opportunity for research, I stood and rather too loudly announced.

'We accept your terms and by our very lives we shall honour them, won't we gentleman?'

I stared at my compatriots; they all nodded their agreement except Elizabeth.

'Elizabeth?' said I.

She looked up and nodded through tear stained eyes.

'Aye well let us have a brew and we'll see about getting you all home.

He made us all a cup of tea (which we all agreed was the worst cup of tea that we had ever had). Then he sat on a large worn out armchair and picked up his cup that was dirtier than the floor.

'This island was discovered many years ago and was quickly realised as being uncharted; a lost island if you will. It was agreed that it must be kept secret. We Scots understood that we had a great discovery and resolved to keep it that way. If people found out about it they would want to hunt and plunder it.

An agreement was made that it would never be disclosed, put on any map or mentioned in any journal or newspaper. That only a very select few could know of its existence. Initially we thought of guarding it but its location serves no real purpose for travel. It is not en route to anywhere except maybe The Arctic.

There was even talk of a diversion. It has been contemplated that we could spread a rumour that there was a monster or dinosaur in one of the lochs on the mainland. This would keep everybody looking inland and in the wrong direction.

My Grandfather was one of the people to be involved with this island outside those who discovered it. It was my grandfather who built this place, my father shared it with me and like him I fell in love. We are what you might call caretakers of this land. We have all the food and drink we need and receive a visit once a month to ensure nothing has gone wrong. If I retire or return to the mainland I will want for nothing as is part of the agreement but the truth is it gets in your blood. I love it ere.'

'Don't you get lonely?' said I.

'Aye, but me and my wife love it.'

'*You have a wife.*' exclaimed Giles.

'*Yes, I bloody do* and don't sound so surprised you cheeky bugger.'

'Apologies sir.' said Giles smiling briefly.

'She is on the mainland at the moment and she doesn't take kind to visitors especially uninvited ones so consider yourself lucky. Now I've lost me thread, well that's who I am and what I am doing here now what about you's?'

We sat back and listened as Giles explained how he had accidentally discovered the place and upon realising it was uncharted arranged for a small expedition. The man looked unimpressed but concluded our tale by introducing himself as Angus.

'How do you keep safe from dinosaurs?' enquired Elizabeth.

'Yes, don't they ever attack the cottage?' said Dean.

'We have a very effective defence.' replied Angus.

'What's that? I haven't seen anything?' remarked Gilbert.

'Yes you have – sand. They hate it and will not step a foot on it.'

'That's why you surrounded the cottage with it. I thought it was a bit odd .'

'Och, you're a quick study.' Angus replied laughing heartily and stroking his great beard.

I remember feeling a flash of anger at the man's continued abruptness.

'How do you make them listen to you?' asked Elizabeth leaning forward.

'They do initially but they are not domesticated. I can get away with it because they are familiar with me but if I was to hang about as sure as anything I would be like your friends back there.'

He read the look of horror that crossed our faces upon hearing such an insensitive remark.

'Apologies ... I guess my social graces have been lost somewhat over the years. Maybe it's better if I show you. Follow me.'

I made a note to myself to be careful of this man visiting London. He would be considered most rude and disagreeable. We followed him through another room which was a lot cleaner and pleasant. We realised the room we had been in was essentially a porch.

There was another room that seemed to be a scientific study. Finally, we went down a small corridor into a box room and were greeted by a most remarkable sight. In a large cage were five baby dinosaurs. They reminded me somewhat of baby eagles with their claws and terrifying face. Their dark grey skin was apparent through the smattering of orange and black feathers that were starting to show.

'Remarkable.' said I.

'That it is. I feed them, look after them, och I even fuss the blighters then just before they become unmanageable I release them onto the island.'

'But how do you get them in the first place?' asked Giles who was hunched at the enclosure making notes and drawing diagrams.

'With a lot of courage and a lot of scotch.'

We all laughed at this remark.

'Aye but it's worth it, with that and a stick of fire you can give yourself just long enough to get away.'

He motioned for us all to leave and albeit each one of us hoped that he would stop in the nicer room he continued leading us back into the porch. We took the same seats as before as if we were children being escorted back to class.

'Is your boat ok?' asked Angus.

'Yes it is fine.' said I 'we came from the direction of the Isle of Lewes.'

'Well, you must be going if you have a boat that works ya cannae stay here.'

'Ok we shall leave your fair isle, but you must allow us to return we are scientists after all.' said Giles.

'And eminent ones at that.' added Gilbert.

'I understand, contact Gerald Hinxworth, Scottish minister of environment, tell him you met me and say you need to talk him for nautical reasons. I expect you'll hear the shock in his voice. And I'll even give you a parting gift, but I do not expect to see you unless you have had permission beforehand. I will go and fetch the souvenir I have in mind for you.'

'Thank you we will wait here. Elizabeth make sure you're ready ... Elizabeth ... *where is Elizabeth?*' cried Gilbert.

Gilbert got up and storm back through the cottage shouting her name. She was just coming out of the box room when she met her father.

'*What the hell are you doing child?*'

'Sorry father, I couldn't tear myself away from the babies, they are so cute.'

'Stay by my side will you until we get home and give me that infernal bag I will carry it for you.'

'I am quite capable father, thank you.' Elizabeth responded marching off ahead.

Back in the reception room Angus returned with a large orange and black feather.

'Thank you but we already have one.' said Giles.

'Do we?' returned I.

'Confound it, we must have lost it in the confusion.' said Dean.

'Aye, that you did.' said Angus beaming a huge smile.

Angus marched us back to our boat via the beach. As we journeyed home grief for our colleagues and friends was finally allowed forward. We had a brief stop in Edinburgh to refresh ourselves. Everyone was off their food except for Elizabeth who ordered extra; we put it down to her being out of sorts.

Upon our return to London, it was agreed that we should all meet on the morrow after plenty of rest. I believe each one of us fell into a long deep sleep full of dinosaurs and lost worlds. Unbeknownst to Gilbert while he was in his slumber his daughter Elizabeth crept downstairs and helped herself to some cured meat. After putting it on a plate, she returned to her bedroom, carefully opened her large leather bag and gently lowered a slice of meat into it. A small snout lined with sharp teeth came out and took it from her.

'Don't worry, mummy will look after you.' she said.

The Magic Circle

The lights were extinguished, and into a dark, lifeless void, the giant creature fell. The beast simply seemed to vanish. What was once so friendly and smiling was now dark and foreboding.

'Really Geoffrey, must we always be last to exit the public house, it is becoming rather embarrassing, our sobriety will be called into question.'

The tall man in a top hat turned to his compatriot, swishing his cloak and pointing his cane he spoke with confidence. 'Nonsense I shall have none such gibber tonight, we are in fine mood and besides the only thing of great concern is whether we make the blasted underground.'

'What difference does that make?'

'The difference is whether my wife will still be with me on the morrow.'

'Edward, you exaggerate.' said he looking at his friend with curious eyes.

'Confound your cavalier attitude.' Edward replied vexed. The rotund man looked florid and out of breath as he hurried his steps to keep pace with his friend's dashing strides.'

They soon loomed upon Bishopsgate with its well-worn paths and roads and dashed into the station, 'Hold all trains my good fellow.' cried Geoffrey. They both stopped in their tracks and were astonished by what they saw.

'I cannot see a living soul. What on earth has happened to everyone?'

'It is most peculiar but we still need to make haste. If we miss the last train we shall be very late indeed.'

The pair raced down the corridors. Geoffrey was faring better than Edward who was panting heavily. They reached the bottom expecting to come upon a crowded platform which was usual for the last train on a Friday night. The gas light was dimmer than usual against the acrid black smoke that hung in the air like a malevolent phantom, the station was empty, devoid of human life. It appeared to be abandoned.

'Where is this confounded monstrosity of a train?'

'You don't suppose the station is closed do you?'

'No I do not Geoffrey, this is most irregular, it has me rather on edge.'

'Nonsense Edward, there is nothing to fear we are at Bishopsgate Station the forefront of British Engineering, I hardly think there is anything to fear old man.'

'We shall see.'

'Listen, I can hear the great beast coming now I am sure she shall be full to the brim.'

The giant steam engine pulling lantern lit carriages rumbled slowly into view and there was a look of relief on the men's faces at the sign of humanity. It roared into the station loud and clumsy like a drunkard fumbling for keys at his front door.

There was not a single soul aboard.

'*Good grief Edward*, this is eerie.' Geoffrey turned to look at Edward as he said it and noticed that his pallor had turned from rose to flour. '*What is it man? You look like you have seen a ghost.*'

'*No one was driving the train!*'

'Have you gone mad Edward? Of course someone was driving the train.'

'I tell you Geoffrey there was no one at the helm.'

'Well we must get aboard otherwise the vexation of my wife will be unbearable. It was probably a trick of the light, there are more shadows down here than objects, I am sure of it.'

The two men stepped aboard the wooden carriage. It was empty there was not even a discarded broadsheet or a neglected scarf.

The train chugged noisily out of the station, black smoke consumed the outside and the gas lighting created a nauseous miasma within.

'Maybe all will be well,' said Edward taking a seat and placing his top hat on the bench. Geoffrey took the seat opposite and mimicked his actions.

'Confound you Edward, really. Of course, we shall be safe.

'Does this infernal machine usually travel so fast?' Geoffrey said as they both peered out of the window together.

'It must be light and shadow again my dear boy; we can't possibly be travelling at the speed it appears as it is a scientific impossibility.' as Geoffrey finished saying it his mouth dropped open as a station whizzed by as if it was nothing but a ghostly whisper dancing in the night.

'That could not have been Edward, I tell you.'

'It was as I say man, something peculiar is afoot, I know it is.'

'Perhaps we should have a drink to calm our nerves.' said Geoffrey pulling a small flask of whisky out of his coat and offering it to his friend, he gladly took a big swig.

The ghostly wisps kept on flying by at an ever rapid rate.

'But it cannot be we are out of stations.' cried Geoffrey, taking a huge gulp of his drink and returning it to his coat with unsteady hands.

The station ghosts kept on flying by. *'What is this trickery? I demand an answer.'* bellowed Edward standing up. There was no response to his courageous outburst and he sat back down.

'We cannot worry Edward.' said Geoffrey reading his friends face. 'What will be is inevitable so let us face it like gentlemen and march boldly forward.'

As he finished his sentence the train started slowing down; the pair stared at each other. They looked out into the darkness, but could not see any light, not even a shadow except those within the carriage itself.

'I still cannot see anything Edward?'

'By Jove, look, Geoffrey the other side!' replied Edward, frantically pointing to the other side of the carriage. The men both got up and stared out of the windows on the opposite side, mouths agape. They were pulling into a station, except it wasn't a station as such, it was more like a large cave made out of mud.

The back wall was full of tiny alcoves that created little cubby holes and crudely cut tree's created shelving, they were both filled with strange looking vials, potions and bizarre looking candles. There was a large bar akin to what one would see in a public house stretching out in front of it, but it what was in front of the bar that startled Edward and Geoffrey.

They opened the carriage doors and both men hesitated for a second.

'Construction?' said Geoffrey, slightly losing his nerve.

'Construction man, now it is *you* who has gone mad. I said there was something peculiar about all this.'

'Why hallo there.' said Edward bravely stepping out of the carriage, Geoffrey stepped out in an even bolder fashion and strode past his counterpart. After a couple of steps the Victorian drinkers stopped in their tracks, both a little unsure, for up ahead of them was a small man, well something akin to one.

The creature was about four feet high and covered in wiry brown hair all over its body. The face was just a matt of hair with slivers of pink circling the eyes and mouth, its teeth looked humanoid but were rounded and a slightly odd shape, the feet of the creature were undecipherable as too much hair sprouted out of them covering everything. The creature was dressed in a white shirt, red waistcoat and what appeared to be tailored trousers.

The two men looked at each other telepathically discussing the risk to life. The creature may have been a deal shorter than them, but they did not know their quarry. Both men agreed that caution was prudent, just as they were about to verbally affirm their thoughts, a strange voice snapped them out of their stupor.

'Hallo Gentlemen, why come forward, it is your lucky night, tonight is the extravaganza.'

The men looked at each other and then walked forward tentatively.

'You speak English?' enquired Geoffrey.

'You speak?' asked Edward.

'Of course I speak gentlemen, please come forward, I mean you no harm, why do people always react to me this way?' the creature replied, gesturing with a furry paw within which small pink digits could just about be made out.

'What sort of creature are you?'

'Please Gentleman, you have no time for questions now, the train will be leaving shortly. This is a shop, but not like any other in this world, you may pick any bottle you like and drink its contents, you are guaranteed a surprise worth your money. The price is half a crown regardless of the one you choose.'

'Half a crown sir, I say that is robbery in the most blatant terms.' said Geoffrey holding his cane up slightly to accentuate his point.

'Underground London is a magical place and you have stumbled upon us at the height of our festivities. The price is usually a full crown, but I must warn you no one has stumbled upon me twice.'

The two men glanced at each other suspiciously.

'Gentlemen please, it was not a threat, I told you I meant no harm and I meant it. I am a tradesman that is all.' the creature said holding out his arms in a pleading gesture.

'So what is it exactly that you sell?' asked Edward.

'Experience, my good sir, experience is what I sell.' the furry being replied.

'How extraordinary.' Edward repeated, rubbing his chin and finally starting to relax in the creatures company.

'You mean Opium?' enquired Geoffrey.

'Certainly not, there is no magic in that sir I assure you, now come, you must be quick. Pick one. Look at your surroundings, magic is in the air, any man of wisdom can see it.'

'This is most singular Geoffrey, we are either in some strange world or one of us is asleep on the train and dreaming, in either case there is no point in not continuing our adventure.'

'I agree Edward we shall not retreat, but I am suspicious of skulduggery.'

'Geoffrey, the train moved at speeds which hitherto has only been in the dreams of scientists and young boys. Here is my money good man.' said Edward walking forward and placing the half-crown in the creature's hands. He saw small pink uncooked sausages take the coin from amidst the fur.

'Yes ok then, here you go good fellow.' Geoffrey said adding a half-crown to the other open palm.

'Excellent gentlemen, this will be the most exquisite, fantastic and memorable experience of your lives and that of the generations to come as well I suspect.' the little creature jumped really high and let out a girlish squeal patting his hands together with incredible speed.

'What an odd little creature you are.' said Geoffrey.

'I live for the underground you see sir and love to share its warmth with all, it doesn't come finer than a little Bishopsgate magic I assure you. Now pick. You haven't much time.'

'But there are so many how are we supposed to choose?' stated Edward.

'*I know, I know, isn't it great.*' the creature yelped jumping up and down again.

'We better decide Geoffrey.'

'What about that one there Edward, it looks so peculiar, the purple mixture glows as if it is alive.' Geoffrey said, pointing to one of the bottles.

'You certainly have decided on an adventure.' said Edward, 'that it is the most peculiar bottle I have ever laid eyes upon.'

The creature did not even wait for confirmation, it ran around the back of the bar, pulled out a ladder made of sticks and hessian, ran up it, grabbed the bottle and raced back leaving the ladder where it was.

'Here gentleman, a mouthful each, quick.' the creature handed Edward the bottle.

It had a bulbous glass bottom with a myriad of glass triangle shards, the bottle then split into two pipes and reconnected to make the lip. The strange purple concoction glowed enticingly.

Edward took a large mouthful and quivered. He looked at his counterpart and nodded. Geoffrey took the bottle and gulped a large mouthful. Both men expressed surprise.

'What an odd sensation, it is like I have drunk electricity, laced with alcohol and a fruit that I cannot describe.'

'Why, I am tingling all over.' Edward replied with a surprised look on his face.

'You must depart now, but remember *you must come back today*.' said the creature still rubbing his furry paws with glee.

'*Today?* – What a remarkable thing to say. This is the last train!'

'Be off with you my friends. The train will leave any second.' the creature said in a firm tone that was somehow still laced with pleasantry.

It was only then that the men became aware that the light faintly coming from the carriage behind had now grown bright.

They slowly turned around and were astonished to see a strange snakelike beast emitting bright light behind them. It had a large red streaks running down its body and bright amber lights. Suddenly its belly opened up and they saw what looked like bright yellow ribs within.

'What can it be Edward?' said Geoffrey, leaning forward refusing to walk any closer.

'Look at the orange pattern within - confound it, it is writing Edward, this is no beast, it is some kind of carriage.'

'*Hurry, hurry before the doors close.*' the familiar voice came from behind.

The men ran aboard now convinced of their safety. They stood there mesmerised by the digital readout and the futuristic, spacious and comfy design.

'*Mind the Doors.*' a siren sang in a smooth tone.

'Who said that? There is no one here. What is this devilry? This cannot be of our age surely.' said Geoffrey stamping his cane onto the floor.

'Where can we be going?' said Edward looking at the orange words painted in light, 'there is no station called Liverpool Street and look at this map Geoffrey, Bishopsgate is not even upon it, what is this madness?'

'*Look, a Newspaper*!' said Geoffrey running down the carriage to where the paper lay upon a seat. He picked it up and his mouth dropped wide open. 'My dear fellow, I believe we have stumbled upon an adventure indeed, look at the date, and more importantly the year.'

Edward was standing behind Geoffrey reading over his shoulder. '*By Jove* – 2018, you mean that this is from the …'

'That is precisely what I mean.' said Geoffrey cutting him off. 'It all makes sense; look at the date.'

'Why, that is a week ago today - of course the creatures's words …' said Edward. As he did, he and Geoffrey turned to each other.

'*You must come back today*!' they said in unison.

'T'is a magical adventure indeed,' said Edward sitting down.

Bleeding Chips

Ready for the gutter was I on that fateful day. On the verge of destitution with my employment lost and my wife and son deceased. Slowly had I witnessed my reflective transformation from a man with pride to a creature of bitterness and despair. There was only one remnant, one minute strand of respectability that still clung to me like a spider's silk, but even that was about to fray.

The strand to which I refer was a gentleman's club located in Chelsea. As one might imagine by its location, it was of the illustrious variety, and I was indeed fortunate to be a member.

A friend's father had gotten me in and paid five years membership on my behalf as his son and I had schooled together and still frequented social gatherings. Alas, my good friend was lost in the heart of India, and it is believed that he was consumed by the mighty *Panthera Tigris* or tiger as it is commonly known. But tragedy had only just begun to dance on my would be grave as my friend's father, with considerable alacrity might I add, followed his son to the grave. Bereavement was just too much for the old fellow.

These events distraught me immensely for these folk were practically my kin, how could I have known that my world had merely shook, soon it would be torn asunder.

After working late I had got home to hear my son crying and alarmed at my son wailing in such a visceral fashion I ran to his aid. Managing to quickly soothe him I went in search of my spouse with vexation painted across me. Upon opening the bedroom door I found her looking as pale and ill as I had ever witnessed; her forehead was almost scalding to touch. I hastened to find a doctor as quickly as I could.

Thinking it was but a fever rest and liquid were prescribed. After a two day absence from work she seemed to recover, returning to work I thought no more of it, but some days later lesions began to appear. Upon hearing my son wail that very same day I found a scalding temperature indistinguishable from the one that had visited my wife. In that single moment I knew in my heart that the pox was about claim my family.

Grief consumed my existence I fell into inebriation and gambling. People tried to convince me of my good fortune for the disease had skirted round me, but it was of little consolation. Once frugal with my finances they became nothing but accessories to my destruction; such was my wanton that I would make bets that only a fool would gamble on and thus it finally came to my attention that I had an addiction.

Finally, it all caught up with me. I was to be evicted from my rooms. My membership of the prestigious club was about to expire and as I could not afford to renew that week's gathering was to be my last. Unfortunately everyone knew it, my friends and peers had silently watched my decline, any intervention was quickly staved off by my own belligerence.

I entered the dimly lit premises, the gaslights gave off their normal yellow hue creating a hazy ambience, only the finest furniture was to be found, men of great stature were often strewn lazily across it as if it were some backstreet opium den.

Walking in I held my head up high and ordered a whisky, and after greeting some of the regulars as if nothing was amiss I headed to the gambling tables. There was renewed vigour in my stride that day and not without reason.

Just the week before a new card game called poker had reached our shores. A bizarre choice of name I agree, what it has to do with my fireplace I shall never discern, intrigued nonetheless I decided I would entertain this most singular card game.

Much to my surprise I really enjoyed it and started winning but I could not stop playing and rapidly lost it all again. Convinced this was an error of alcohol I was determined on this - my last night - to make amends. I would drink less and win the money. Then I would resolve to be more prudent in my affairs and formulate a constructive design for my life.

Confound it, despite containing my inebriation and my best efforts I failed in my task and had nothing to show at the end of it. Hitherto I had watched the looks from the various patrons in the club; their stares had gone from one of empathy to that of pity and judgement. I approached the bar as if being drawn by some spiritual force but had to halt myself halfway for I had foregone my finances.

Upon seeing my predicament the bartender whom I knew well beckoned me over. Whispering in my ear he solemnly informed me that I would have to pay for nothing that night. I thanked him warmly and immediately sought out the mesmerising drunken abyss that creates a jape out of adversity.

It must have been several drinks into the evening that the strange incident occurred. I know this because I can recall the incident yet the warm haze of intoxication had started to affect me; otherwise I should have not taken stock of the man.

As I sat there drinking my next remedy I heard a voice call me:

'Why hallo there sir, will you join me for moment please.'

The bedraggled man who was hailing me was tall and thin wearing what appeared to be a blue suede jacket. A thin white beard adorned his scrawny head as did his thin straggled hair.

'I must apologise but tonight I will be left to my own devices.' I remember raising my glass and going to tip my hat but recalling that I had left with the cloaks.

'Nonsense you must join me my good man. I insist.'

'Sir.' I replied. 'I wish not to be bothered at this time and I would thank you to respect that.' I showed him my back.

The man bellowed at me like I was a petulant child, *'Robert Ian Cople do not turn you back on me!'*

The thing that startled me the most was that he shouted my name - my full name. I had never divulged my middle name to anyone except my late wife.

Astounded, I walked over to him 'how do you know my name, my full name I mean, nobody knows that sir it was not even on the deeds of my house let alone this club.'

The man pushed a bar stool to me using his foot with surprising vigour.

'Take a seat young man and listen to me; now that I finally have your attention.'

The man sipped his beer, I could see golden droplets clinging to the hairs at the side of his mouth, he adroitly wiped them away with his sleeve and began his curious monologue.

'Who I am is not of importance or relevance.'
'What?'
'Silence - you really can be a most a quarrelsome rascal at times if you do not let me finish what I have to say I shall leave you sir and you will be a lot worse off for it.'

The man stared at me intently his thin cheeks flushed red, despite his age there seemed to be strength hiding behind his withered disguise.

'Pray continue.' I replied biting my tongue from saying anything further.

'As I said I know who you are and I know your story. You have fallen on ill times my friend but your fortune is about to change.'

I gasped to speak but his look convinced me otherwise. 'I am a man who has been more successful than his wildest dreams. Just about everything I desired I have owned or experienced, I have travelled the world, dined with scholars and kings and explored the seas and reaped its bounties.'

I recall at the time having the thought that he might be a pirate if there still exists such a thing. The strange man continued with his story:

'My success started with hard work but when I thought I had achieved all I could I was given this.' The old man reached deep in his trouser pocket and fumbled about for a few seconds before pulling out a small blue round disc. For a second I was flummoxed as to what it was but it quickly dawned on me.

'That is one them confounded poker chips that has brought about my ruin this very evening.' said I.

'It is a poker-chip my good sir but I assure you it will bring you good luck – it is a *lucky* chip.'

His voice was stern and clear when he spoke the words lucky chip, his eyes narrowed as if daring me to challenge him, now the mystery had been revealed challenge him I did.

'You waste my time with this old man, brandy has your senses.' replied I as curt as I could.

'Sit down you ruddy fool.' he said pulling me back down onto the stool with considerable force.

'This here will bring you nothing but luck and you my friend are in great need of it. Now for the last time listen to me, if I am some old crazy fool what harm can it do to hear me out for five minutes and take the chip with you, you still have your drink don't you?'

Again the wily old man had me cornered I would only be consuming my drink alone if I left him. I allowed him to continue his discourse but with suspicion in my mind.

'This chip has brought me nothing but luck even though it took me years to realize it. The strange thing was I threw it away on many occasions but it always turned up in the oddest places and at the strangest of times.

Once it even turned up when I was fishing, within minutes of discovering it amongst my tackle I caught the biggest fish I had ever seen, I even had to ask a man on the riverbank to assist me. So enthralled was he by my fishing skills that he asked me to teach him. I accepted but warned him that it had been luck. It turned out that he owns a country estate and normally fishes his own lake he was just trying out the river to see if he could catch anything bigger. To bring this anecdote to a close let us just say that we became firm friends; a few years later he died and left his entire estate to me.'

'Good grief I would say that is good fortune but the reasoning is more logical I assure you. In all likelihood you dropped the chip in your tackle after too much of the old sailor's medicine.'

'I can *assure you* that I have tested that theory on many occasions but all this is not of consequence at the moment. I ask only one question of you - be I a fool or be I not will you accept this gift from me?'

'Yes I will and I thank you for it kind Sir.' my gratitude was sincere for delusional or not his intent was obviously benevolent. He placed the blue chip into my hand.

'What is your name?' I asked.

He pulled a deep blue suede top hat from a stool hidden behind him. 'My name is not important. I bid you farewell I would wish you good luck but I know now that you will not require it.' he placed the hat on his head tipped it slightly at which point I reciprocated with a nod. He then walked out of the establishment with a forthright stroll; not a single person in the club either said goodbye or acknowledged him albeit his suede blue suit was most singular indeed.

I carried on my drinking most people being too embarrassed to drink with me popped by with kind yet patronising words. I pondered my interlocution with the old man and allowed my mind to wonder. As with all drunken stupors, it wasn't long before the mysterious liquor driven time machine whisked me to the next day.

I awoke in my rooms that had already been stripped of most furniture and valuable belongings. There was just my bed, an armchair, my precious desk, that I could not bear to part with, and one dining chair to use at the desk. Numbness overtook me as I realised the day of my destitution had finally arrived.

Bound for the gutter I got up and after fetching myself an early morning drink I pondered my fate. I decided to check my trouser pockets in case of some forgotten fortune. I searched and immediately felt some money in my pocket. It was not much but it would feed me for a few days I then recalled someone giving me charity as I exited the club last night. I made a spectacle of myself but most of them had wished me well.

After spying a bottle of whisky on the floor I remembered the barman telling me I could take it home. Pacing around the room trying to think I ignored the whisky determined to come up with a plan to get my life back on track.

After an hour, I slumped into my single armchair and wept, I sobbed like a little boy. The ghost's of my wife and son endlessly taunted me. I imagined them shaming me for betraying their memories. When I had exhausted my tears I saw the overcoat that I had worn the night before. I searched my pockets. Every pocket was empty; every pocket except one.

I pulled out the blue chip, the so-called *lucky* blue chip, from the previous night. As I stood the crazy old man reappeared in my mind as if he were right in front me. I grew angry and rage began to consume me. The fact that I had allowed myself to be taken in by such a cruel jape combined with the hopelessness of my predicament, like a dormant volcano finally waking from its slumber, I erupted.

I kicked over the chair and pummelled the desk with my fists. I knocked over the armchair then picked up the blue chip and threw it violently in the bin. I walked around the room continually pounding the walls with my fists, screaming angrier than ever, my hands banging on hard wood with soft dull thuds, but then as if I had hit a glockenspiel a much higher note resounded back to me.

My jaw dropped. Immediately I righted my armchair and sat down. I gathered up my whisky bottle, allowed myself one large swig, then I sat back breathing heavily. Later on, I would feel terrific shame for my wanton violence but at that moment only one thing occupied my mind – a hollow section in the wall.

Apologies if you leapt to the wrong conclusion but I already knew it was there, such was the quality of the hiding place that my wife and I had used it instead of a bank to store some savings. Back when my wife was alive I had thrived rather well and she, ever the frugal sort, was adamant that we should have investment for the future. We put aside a considerably large sum as a fall back. We still had plenty of savings in plain sight, as it were, but as you know I managed to squander it all.

The question that weighed so heavily upon me was - had I spent it already? It had been so long that I could not recall whether my wife and me had done anything with it. It may seem strange to a man grown in his confidence but I wanted to be prepared for the right answer. I slowly rose from the chair, deciding that the hiding hole would be empty, loosened the strip of wood and then removed the panel.

I peered inside and immediately saw a large bundle wrapped in letter writing paper; I pulled it out scarcely containing my excitement.

My hands trembled as I sat back down once again in my chair; I opened the paper and found a great wad of bank notes that my wife had been adding to in an earnest fashion. It was then that my thoughts once again returned to the blue chip. Placing the money on the table I felt a mixture of both Joy and foolishness at my own folly. Now I had been given a second chance I got up and picked the chip out of the waste paper basket.

Recalling the old man's story I wondered if it could be true? My initial reasoning seemed logical enough for it was the chip that provoked my uproar and caused physical outburst. If I had not of found it would I have still acted the way that I did? Whilst there was a chance, would I have struck the same panel? The hollow was small and singular yet I felt I had no chance but to dismiss such a fantastical tale. I smiled as I thought of the old man bearing witness to these events and his would be jubilant reaction to them.

Turning my attention to finances I made some plans; I would pay my rent and renew my membership at the club. Finally, I picked the bottle of whisky off the floor and threw it in the bin. Then I placed the chip in secret hiding place for safe keeping.

The next day I dressed as a gentlemen would and strolled through the street with my head held high in the air. I placed my money in the bank so that it would be safe. This unexpected monetary surprise had galvanised me to honour the memory of my family and act for the better.

I decided to trick myself into my new way of life by breakfasting in an eloquent establishment. I found such a parlour with nice tables outside, and the sun was shining as if a promise of good things to come. Such was my mood that even the continuous clopping of horses, the rattling of hansoms and dogcarts did not fray my patience as usual.

I had treated myself to a paper with the hope of inspiration as I placed it on the table my eyes happened upon an advertisement:

'*CRUISE TO AMERICA FOR ADVENTURE AND INSPIRATION*'

'By Jove, that is the answer.' cried I. After examining the price and details I surmised it was of good value. As much as drink and gambling had done their bit my grief was still there and I wondered whether this could serve as the perfect antidote. The shop that had advertised it was nearby so after finishing my tea I strolled briskly there with the paper folded under my arm.

I walked into the tiny store and approached the tall gaunt man at the counter. I rifled through my pocket to get out some money and amongst the coins I felt something odd. It was the same shape as a coin but bigger and a completely different texture. Flabbergasted was I when a blue poker chip came out of pocket.

I had placed the lucky chip in my hidey hole for safe keeping so I examined it but the same blemishes were in all the correct locations – it was my lucky blue chip. Feeling the proprietor's agitation and impatience I proudly announced to the man that I wish to book myself on his advertised wondrous cruise.

'Terribly sorry sir but it is no longer available.' said the man shrugging his shoulders genially.

'What on earth do you mean?'

'This offer is so cheap because the company *BlackSun Cruises* and their ship are new; it sold out not twenty minutes ago.'

'Blast,' I cursed. Opening my hand I looked at the blue chip, 'lucky indeed' I thought to myself with more than a little sarcasm. 'Is there not a reservation list?'

'Not that I am aware of but I can take your details and if someone should cancel, which I would find highly unlikely given that it sails in a few days.'

'When does it sail?'

'Wednesday two O'clock from the docks. I will send word to you immediately if there is a cancellation I promise.'

'That sounds good enough to me sir.' said I tipping my hat at him. 'Have you not got some other cruise that you can offer?' asked I as I wrote down my particulars.

'That I have but at prices that would offend you. The *BlackSun* one was remarkably cheap you must understand. The only similar trip I have is at least double the price and not as extensive either.' The man looked at me with hollow eyes. I let out a loud sigh and walked out of the shop.

Once I was home I pulled the blue chip out of my pocket and placed it firmly on the table. Then I checked my hiding place the chip was gone. Sitting down I threw my face into my hands flummoxed. It was impossible it could not be the same chip. There was no explanation, in the end I settled on agreeing with myself that I might fathom it at a later date.

This chip was certainly not lucky though I began to reason that I would have found that money in any case. Bitterly disappointed that my new start was halted so abruptly I hit upon an idea. Using my pocketknife I carefully I etched into it the initials of wife on one side and the initials of my deceased child on the other. The letters were engraved nice and deep, I picked up the blue chip, walked out into my back garden and there I threw it as hard as I could across the neighbour's yards. Confident that there could be no chance of co-incidence now I returned to my abode and retired for the night.

A few days later, I awoke realising that I had not slept that well in a long time. The morning shone bright, I opened my windows wide, the freshness of sleep had also rejuvenated my attitude. Deciding to forget my false start I set myself to thinking about what I could do with my money in order to secure myself a future.

Little did I know that the most peculiar adventure was about to happen upon my doorstep. There was a knock on my door which I duly answered. I encountered a rotund middle-aged man who was clean-shaven in smart dress with a cane and greasy black parted hair.

The man stood there staring at me.

'Can I help you Sir.' enquired I.

The man's face had reaction and it seemed ambivalent as if both surprised and offended. The man continued staring at me as if he were a mannequin in a shop window. Just as I was about to threaten the man with Queensbury rules I had the inkling to examine him further. His slightly bulbous nose, his thickened lips and bushy black eye brows, there was something familiar in it all. Suddenly he smiled and at last I knew the reason for his silence.

'*Harold Shillington, how the devil are you man?*'

Then he guffawed his raucous laugh. 'Do forgive me, I was curious as to how long it would take you to recognise me, it has been some years has it not?'

'Indeed it has been many.' replied I.

'I apologise for leaving it so long old friend.' he said putting his hand on my back.

'I will not hear of it I am as much to blame. One thing does strike me as curious though, how did you know where I lived?'

'You remember old George Kempston who used to live down the street from us?'

'Why yes, I am still in touch with him from time to time.'

He raised his eyebrows at me in a mischievous manner.

'Ah I see it was George.' said I.

He guffawed loudly.

'You still have the same terrible laugh then Harold.'

'Shut it you old dog.' he said playfully punching my arm. I was transported back to a time when we used to play fight like ruffians but resisted the urge to respond.

'Well do come in old chap.' we walked through the hallway into my rooms.

'Good grief old man are you moving or something? Please do not inform me that this is all you own after George boasted of how well you are doing.'

'When exactly did you last see old George.'

'I suppose it must have been a few years; took a gamble you see - that you still lived here I mean.'

I recall the gambling comment causing me to snigger briefly. 'I think you better take a seat my old friend there is much we have to discuss, and please take the armchair.'

He sat down. I pulled round the chair from my writing desk and sat down opposite him, then he informed me of his life hitherto, the endless affairs, liaisons and business ventures that he had embarked upon. When it was finally my turn he listened intently to my discourse.

I told of my love for my wife and child and how extremely happy we were, my wealth and social life, how it all began to unravel with the death of my wife and child. I explained in detail my gradual decline in to the abyss of alcoholism and gambling. His eyes moistened softly as I spoke.

He placed his hand on my knee after I had finished. 'I am truly sorry for your woe my old friend, I had no idea, why on earth didn't you reach out to me? I would have been there for you.'

'Thank you, the truth is I would not have accepted anything as nothing could stop me from my path of self destruction.'

'I see your point.' he said leaning back.

'Pray forgive if I seem discourteous but did you pop round just to catch up after years of procrastination?' enquired I with a warm smile.

'Ah yes, that my friend is a bit of a tricky one.'

'How so?'

'Well, I actually came round to offer you a business proposal.'

'I have recently found some money that I forgot I had and it is enough to invest in a new life so any business proposal you have is of the greatest interest to me.'

'I am pleased to hear that my old friend, you remember my cousin William?'

'Yes I remember him.' said I stroking my chin.

'We have kept in touch and he recently approached me with a business proposition. He was saying that down on the dock there are multitudes of workers and people coming from overseas and passing through yet there is no public house to greet them.'

'*A public house, are you mad, what would I do with a public house?*'

'Hear me out, you would not be running it in fact you would have very little to do with it. The building we have chosen has been researched to the nth degree. The people of the area and passers through by a vast majority want a drink and food establishment on the docks once again. William even has someone lined up to turn the lace as he is no publican neither.'

'I have invested because it makes sense the building used to be pub, but it fell into ruin when the owner died.'

'Yes I remember *The Cat's Tail* it was a hive of ruffians and the number of violent skirmishes there was staggering.'

Harold exhaled and leant forward. 'You are my friend I trust you implicitly, you are still the same man underneath it all I can tell, there is something happening that no one can know … well not yet anyway.'

'Oh, what is that?' asked I sitting upright in my chair.

'There are going to be constables posted very close by.'

'Elaborate.' replied I.

'What you say is true and stopping short of hiring mercenary's to protect the place he knew he had to do something about it.'

'So what has he done?' said I throwing my hands up in frustration.

'William has been having secret meetings all over the docks, reporting crimes and being a bit of a spokesperson for the community with the single aim of proving how dangerous it is. He managed to get a meeting with the government, and persuaded them that a police presence in the heart of the docklands would immediately half the crime. This would in turn induce more trade and therefore a more profitable economy. He even swayed them into keeping it quiet until the station opens; I have to say I was impressed by his forethought.'

'Interesting, very interesting indeed.' I said leaning back and rubbing my chin.

'William also proposed that we offer the police a heavy discount to keep them coming in and out.'

'Your cousin is shrewd and cunning and the prospect seems a good one.'

'It is but there is need for urgency. We have boarded up the front of the establishment so it looks like they will be offices this way if no one catches on to our idea we will have the monopoly.

We even have a friend that is going to run a big piece in the paper covering the opening of our pub and mentioning the police angle. The whole thing is a guaranteed success.

You are my friend so I will be forthright with you. My cousin has the biggest share, I was supposed to have the rest but I didn't have enough to cover it all so we needed to bring a third party in, we wanted someone that we could trust and you sprang immediately to mind.'

'What are the finer particulars?'

'My cousin has fifty percent, I have thirty five and you will own the final fifteen percent.'

'How much is required?'

He slipped me a piece of paper with a fairly large figure on it. I had no reason to not to trust him as he made some money from a couple of businesses in the past.

'Harold everything you say sounds plausible, I believe this could be a real pecuniary opportunity and knowing the docks myself I see how a public house in that area would advantageous for a lot of people.'

'Who knows maybe one day the docks will all just be pubs and restaurants.' replied he.

We both looked at each other and burst out laughing at such a preposterous thought.

'Look my old friend we must act as time is of the essence, before he can complete the work we need to show that we have the finances in order gain the contract, do you have the money here now?'

'No, I will need to go to the bank.' I remember thinking what a great opportunity this would be and getting excited about it. I could see me myself strolling through the pub and greeting our customers, introducing myself and entertaining them. 'When does he need the money by?'

'Today.' he responded nervously playing with his hands.

'*Today!*' I exclaimed. I realised this venture was wholly reliant on my participation and wondered if I might improve my standing by using it as leverage, especially as I wanted to have more say in the decision making from now on.

'Am I correct in stating that there will be plenty of paperwork to corroborate the deal?'

'There are plenty of documents and you can gladly view whatever you like, we have nothing to hide.'

'Let us go this afternoon then.' said I about to suggest that we take luncheon together.

'*Good grief no.*' he ejaculated. 'We must be there one o'clock sharp. And then Michael has to get our signed documents and our money to a meeting by the docks at two.'

'You know I get the feeling of *déjà vu* Harold; I'm sure there was something I was supposed to be doing today.'

'Well there certainly is now my friend, what time is it anyway?'

'Twelve forty-five.' replied I.

'No it is not, don't be so obtuse man, it is not even twelve I doubt.' he said pulling out his pocket watch. 'You see eleven thirty-five.'

'I fear your clock has stopped.'

'No my friend it is yours that has I assure you.'

'Well mine is still ticking.' said I holding my silver pocket watch up to my ear.

He held his up to his ear and I watched his face change as he shook it violently and then put it back to his ear.

'*Confound it.*' he said leaping out of his chair. '*We must go now.*'

We hastened out the door and flagged down a handsome and albeit we paid the man to not spare the whip by the time I had popped into the bank we arrived fifteen minutes late at the office.

'Hopefully my cousin is still here. Have you all the money ready?'

'Yes.' I replied.

'You're sure.'

'Yes.' I replied. Rather annoyed I stuck my hand in my pocket and my face turned ashen white.

'By Jove, what on earth is the matter old man, have you lost it?' he looked as concerned as me.

The money was in my pocket but there was also the now familiar feel of a small round disc on my fingers. I pulled it out not wanting to look, it could not be I had specifically marked it and threw it away into my neighbour's yard. If this does not have the markings then I will have myself a clue thought I while trying to mimic a detective story that I had recently read in *the strand* magazine.

Slowly, I pulled out the disc and examined it. It was my lucky blue chip, I was looking at my wife's initials scribed by my hand, I turned it over and found myself reading my sons initials.'

'Confound you man, what bothers?'

I looked up at him. 'The money is safe, but there is something else that I dare not speak of lest you think me a fool or a madman.'

'Don't be so ridiculous; I think that already.' he guffawed so loud it caused me to wince. 'Now come on you can tell me in a minute we are late already.' he said marching off down an alley.

I felt little anxious as the alley was quite dark and for a moment I wondered whether a group of ruffians were about to conveniently mug me. We approached a brown wooden door with a window next to it. I peered through the glass and saw that it was a small office. The proprietor of the building had obviously been opportunistic by creating a small business space to rent out.

Harold was banging the on the door. 'Blast it we have missed him.' he said.

'Harold if you look through the window you will observe that is obvious.'

'Well come.' he said that he must be at the docks by two o'clock and not a second later.'

'Why?'

'He has an important meeting at the pub should we get there in time we can save the deal, you might as well know that he was trying to barter for an extension, although it was highly unlikely.'

We ran to the street, flagged down the first hansom we saw and sped our way across the city. The hansom driver delivered us right to the property on the waterfront, we leapt out, there was a hive of activity ships coming in and out, loading and unloading. I saw immediately that there could be no doubt of an eager and huge demand for custom. I wanted to handover my money with alacrity.

I looked up at our building, the brick was dirty and sullied from years of standing by the docks. We approached the door and Harold violently wriggled the handle but I could see that it was locked.

'Confound it I don't have a key; he must be in here.' Harold started slapping the door with his hand. '*Michael, Michael open up it's Harold.*'

There was no answer, just silence.

'*Blast what is with the man.*' cried Harold walking to one of the large wooden boards covering the front window. He walked over and started banging his fists on the board.'

'Michael, Michael, open up confound it, it is I Harold.'

'*Stop it Harold.*' I yelled.

Harold stopped and looked at me. I leant my ear to the front door and listened intently, there was not a sound.

'There is no one in there, I cannot hear a sound, if there is a group of people in there it is highly unlikely we would not hear anything whatsoever.'

'Of course he is in there he said he was going to the docks; he just can't hear us.'

'*Michael, Michael, Michael.*' Harold yelled now smashing his plump fists on the board as hard as he could.

'*What the hell do you think you are doing Sir?*' shouted a curly, grey haired man angrily shaking a gold tipped cane at us. He came walking our way with such vexation I wondered whether a physical altercation might immediately ensue.

'I might advise you to mind your own business, but I am trying to get someone's attention who is in the building. There is nothing to fear as I own the building in any case.'

I watched as the strangers face blurted out sounds of astonishment and indignation; his face turned crimson.

'What is the meaning of this Sir? I shall call the police and strike you myself, how dare you?' The man lifted his cane to strike.

Harold curled his big fist up and raised it. '*You dare to threaten me?*'

'Gentlemen, gentlemen, we are dignified men are we not?' said I dashing over to get in between them.

'Then what is the meaning of this pretence that you own the building – when the building belongs to me and in its entirety might I add.'

It was now Harold's turn to look flabbergasted. 'No Sir, this cannot be my cousin has arranged to buy this establishment and I have bought into it as my good friend here is about do also.'

The man stamped his gold tipped cane on to the pavement in protest at what he was hearing.

'And what may I ask is your cousins name?'

'Michael.' responded Harold holding the man's eye contact.

'*Michael*.' the man laughed. 'Michael? His surname would not be Shillington by any chance?'

'Why yes it would?' answered Harold now looking rather astonished. 'How do you know?'

I remember sinking my head in my hand waiting for the inevitable.

The stranger softened his face and took off his hat. 'My good Sir, my name is Arthur Hatch.' he extended his leather glove covered hand.'

'Harold, Harold Shillington.' said Harold looking confused as he took the hand of his interlocutor.

I shook his hand as well but he did not take my name.

'Michael Shillington has been in my employ for some months now as project manager for the renovation of this building. I am seeking him urgently as he has had a lot of money from me and has not being paying the contractors as he was supposed to.'

'I know all about the renovation, a new public house, I have even been inside, the police are going to relocate down here making it safe for night time punters once again and there is an establishment being prepared them around the corner as we speak.'

'Good grief, he has told you everything.'

'Arthur, there must be some mistake I have seen all the paperwork and have also seen his name and signature on the deed.'

'I assure you Harold you are wrong, tell me did you closely examine and read the documents or did he just show them to you flashing his name and signature.'

'Well he ... uh ... well I didn't really examine them as such, what are you implying?'

'His name and signature are indeed upon the documents but as a witness as he was in my employ when I first bought the place. Ironically, it was at that moment that I decided to ask him to be the project manager. The man has had many hundreds of pounds off me that was meant for building work. I have just learned that he has being using credit in my name and keeping the cash for himself. As the work was being carried out I never suspected a thing, but yesterday one of the stores sent me a telegram as the owner knows that I do not like using credit. He thought it was odd that I should be running up such a large bill after years of paying up front. I immediately started making enquiries all across town and discovered what I believed to be a nefarious web of malpractice.'

I watched as Harold's face began to sink.

'But what about the police moving down to the docks and all the community action?'

'Harold I dread to tell you that I think his genius has been that he has only told you one lie.'

'That it was his.' I grimaced.

'Yes exactly my friend for everything he has told you about Harold is absolutely true, but it has been me doing all the deals and community action, and as he is project manger there was absolutely no information that he was not privy to.' said Arthur leaning forward and gently placing his hand on his arm.

Several loud shrills of ships whistle startled us all, I pulled out my pocket watch and glanced up at the time, it was just after two.

'*Of course, two O'clock Wednesday, quick, to the docks.*' cried I.

Harold looked bemused but Arthur's face lit up like a little boy on Christmas Morning.

'*The conniving sneak.*' said Arthur stamping the ground with his cane with such ferocity that I thought he must have fractured it.

'*What is it?*' cried Harold grabbing my shoulders.

'My dear fellow don't you see, there was no meeting after the pub. Michael was going have us sign a load of fake documents take the money and then he was coming to the docks to catch a ship, the *BlackSun* cruise leaves at two o'clock for America, I should know I was supposed to be on it.'

'That's why he was so implicit about to the final handover on his own.' Harold buckled over and put his hands on knees.

'I suppose he must have figured it was too risky to wait any longer and he already had stolen enough money from me in any case.' said Arthur clenching his fist. 'It is too late to go after the ship though as it sounds its horn as it pulls out of the dock.'

'I tell you the truth, I have had many a business venture and have experienced my fair share of losses, but never would I suspect that own kin seek to harm me.' said Harold with moistened eyes.

'Money corrupts too many people; I did not get to my position without witnessing it numerous times. Forgive me for being personal but has he taken you for much?'

'Five hundred pounds.' replied Harold.

'*Five hundred.* By Jove he has stolen enough to live like a king for the rest of his life, no wonder he fled to America, but he will not escape that easily I shall send some *Pinkerton's* after him, I swear it.'

'My own cousin how could he do it to me, we grew up together, how has this happened?' Harold was now pacing.

'I am as horrified as you Harold. We were all childhood friends you see.' said I turning to Arthur.

'Well this much I will say, the public house opens next Thursday and you are both invited as honoured guests. Everything shall be free and you can eat and drink as much you like. I shall of course make paperwork available for inspection in the back office so you can satisfy yourselves that it all is as I say. Policemen will be attending so you can even have me arrested if I am lying. Finally, I shall send the best detectives after this man. Should they recoup any of the money I shall return half of all I recover back to you until your five hundred pounds has been fully returned. That is the best I can offer I am afraid.'

'That is very generous of you sir and I gladly accept, we will both happily attend your launch as well.'

'Yes I concur.' added I.

'Excellent, well I shall see you both there. I wish we had met upon better circumstances but as you can imagine I have a lot to attend to.'

'Yes, I myself will hasten back to the bank to return my money.' said I.

'I will accompany you.' said Harold.

'Gentlemen, please take one of my hansoms, back on the road you will see a line of them waiting just mention my name and they will take you wherever you like.'

We thanked him and after shaking hands, we departed. As we walked up the road I suddenly recalled the blue chip. I began to think that old man had tricked me into accepting a curse. First, I could not take my sabbatical trip and now it I was nearly left in ruins, but there lie the hole in my theory. I didn't lose anything perhaps I had actually been saved. There was no way that I had collected the chip from the neighbours garden as I still remained sober. I gently pulled on Harold's arm and led him back to the water.

'My friend, I have an odd request to make.'

'After today's affairs, I will do anything.' he said without jest.

I led him back to the waterfront and pulled the blue chip out of my pocket, I passed it to him to inspect. The smell of stagnant water and fish coursed through our noses like saw blades. We could see the ship that had escaped us in the distance still dwarfing skiffs alongside it.

'What is it old chap?' he asked looking at what was to him a peculiar object.

'That is a poker chip.' said I.

'What kind of absurdity is a poker chip.'

'Essentially it replaces a coin in betting. Poker is a new American card game; I will show you it sometime but be warned its addiction can be devilry.' said I looking at him earnestly.

'I have no interest in cards, never have.' he said emphatically as he straightened his waistcoat.

'Nonsense, you used to love it when were young.'

'When we were young maybe. What are these initials on either side of the coin?'

'They are those of my wife and child, now listen here all I want you to do is witness me throwing it into the river.'

Harold looked at me as if I had gone mad. He scratched his head.

'I was addicted to gambling.' said I giving him a look so that he would think it was because of my former gambling problem. It worked, he gave a small cough and apologised. I held it up then threw the chip as hard I could into the river.

'Do you feel better?' Harold asked.

I replied that I did but was wondering whether I should see the chip again. The question of my sanity arose in my mind, maybe the drink had done more damage to me than I thought, yet this did not matter now as I had a sober and reliable witness.

We approached a hansom and after giving the cryptic sentence we were whisked to the door of the bank.

'Why are these blasted queues always so long in these places?' said Harold. 'I am in no mood for it today I shall tell you.'

'That does not surprise me, it was simply dread-'

The loud slam of the door hitting the wall startled Harold but not as much as the three men that burst in waving guns and wearing handkerchiefs over their faces.

'*Nobody better bleedin move.*'

'You scoundrels,' cried a sliver haired woman.

One of the men walked forward to raise his gun and hit her with it but stopped short. '*Shut it spinster or you'll be eating lead.*'

I remember thinking that he must have been reading some of those *Wild West* comics that were becoming ever more popular. Without hesitating, I slyly took Harold's cane from him. Harold stared at me incredulously.

'*They have guns.*' he whispered.

One of the gang was already clearing out the tellers draw and I knew they would want the safe. I thought of my wife and child and my blood boiled at the thought of letting down their memory a second time.

A young man stepped forward to confront them and this time the masked man had no hesitation. He cracked his skull hard with the butt of the gun, blood poured immediately and the man fell screaming to the ground.

'*Confound you to hell.*' shouted I.

As I charged at him he did the inevitable. I heard rather than saw the gunshot; the explosion was so loud. I felt the bullet punch my chest, I flew through the air, I knew my time had come - I landed hard on my back. Three shrill blows of a whistle; a policeman was on to them. Turning my head, I saw one of the villains dashing out the door with a small sack in his hand. 'At least they never got to the safe' was my last thought … well at least it should have been.

I heard a man pushing his way through the throng of people that had now surrounded me. '*Come out of the way I am a physician.*' the voice yelled.

A doctor's bag hit the floor, I looked up still having trouble breathing and saw a large round face with a grey wispy beard. He tore my jacket open and then my shirt.

'*Good God!*' he shouted.

This was it … was my chest just a huge bloody hole? Had I unknowingly been shot with a hand cannon?

'*Where's the blood?*' cried Harold.

The doctor frantically ran his hand all over my chest and round my side, I saw him turning his attention to my shirt, then to my jacket, then he stopped still and looked at me.

'You will be fine mister.' said he.

'But … I can't breathe. Well, not easily.' I stammered trying to catch my breath.

'You have knocked the wind out of yourself when you fell on your back you bloody great fool.'

Well despite the recent terrifying ordeal, the whole bank erupted into fits of laughter. I have never been so embarrassed, I did not know whether to laugh or cry, dance or run. I found myself laughing out of sheer relief.

I sat up and touched my chest where the bullet had hit, I winced in pain, there was a circular red mark.

'You'll be ok you will probably have mighty bruise and you could even have bruised a rib so you might feel it for a couple of weeks but you will be fine.' the doctor said getting up. I got up with Harold's help and received a round of applause for my troubles.

'You might want to check your jacket pocket sir.' the doctor continued.

'I saw the hole in my breast pocket, slid my hand in and pulled out the blue chip with a bullet embedded right between my wife's initials.'

'*Cor that was lucky.*' said the doctor.

'*I'd say.*' replied I turning to Harold and giving him a wink.

So what happened to me in the end? I ended up a multi-millionaire, met and fell in love with another beautiful woman and we have two wonderful children. I also travelled and set up many a successful business one of which makes Harold and me a lot of money. Do you remember the club I used to frequent? Well I own it now. As for the blue chip, it sits on my mantelpiece in a special display case that I had especially made for it.

When did I decide whether this chip was lucky or cursed? Well if you need any more convincing, after it saved my life, please allow me to regale you with the newspaper headlines that I woke up to the next day.

'*BLACKSUN CRUISE SHIP SINKS ON MAIDEN VOYAGE TAKING ALL SOULS ON BOARD!*'

'It is a lucky chip indeed.' say I.

A Great Exhibition

A few years have passed since you last joined us. I have some bad news I'm afraid reader. Gilbert passed away during the great Cholera epidemic of forty-eight, his infernal daughter Elizabeth has survived though. I sit here reading the broadsheet of how they are moving the great exhibition or perhaps I should say the Crystal Palace to Sydenham in South London. This I know is a falsehood. It is not being moved but rebuilt after it was accidentally demolished - I should know I was there.

One thing I neglected to inform you of last time I regaled you with my adventures was that Gilbert was extremely wealthy. Albeit he betrothed money to the families of Andrew and Humphrey as well as some to myself, Giles and Dean, Elizabeth was still left immensely rich. She has become a scientist in her own right yet now considered as somewhat eccentric. We have all made numerous trips back to the Hebrides and are now firm friends with Angus and his wife Fenella.

It turns out that unbeknownst to us all Elizabeth had a huge factory style barn built in a field just North of London. Unfortunately for her and the rest of the city some thieves had noticed her continual trips out to its location and burdened with curiosity and the hope of a good score they followed her out there. They came upon the heavily locked giant doors but being masters of their craft managed to gain access - an act that they would live to regret.

Meanwhile myself, Giles and Dean now all a little older were a lot more successful after backing each other up on our paleontological theories. The exhibition was exactly as it was named; great in every way. The forefront of modern science and invention, the place was alight with strange sounds, sights, and even smells. Exotic animals, weird machines and bizarre inventions. It was an absolute marvel.

It was warm inside and the sound of machinery, man and animal combined into an esoteric orchestra for your ears. The aroma's equally competed for dominance, one minute it was grease and oil, then it was the funk of a caged animal and then the sweet smell of a food vendor. We walked around with huge smiles on our faces. I felt lucky to be alive at such a moment in history with Queen Victoria on the throne and all this wondrous technology and advancement.

We were viewing an exotic cat from South America when we first became aware of a commotion. Dean who had tidied up his blond hair and shaved off his goatee leaving only the moustache was trying to coax the cat toward him.

'What is it called?' he asked.
'I believe it is a Jaguar.' replied I.

'Look at the pattern on its coat, simply marvellous.' remarked Giles, his hair had now started to thin, the moustache was still there, but the spectre of age was marching upon him.

As we stood there taking in this beautiful creature, we heard a cacophony of screams in the distance and thought little of it but it continued in the background like an irritating song.

'*What is that infernal racket?*' Giles finally ejaculated.

'Part of the show I imagine.' mused Dean.

Something inside gnawed at my instinct like a rat on bloodied rope.

'That sounds like genuine screams to me as if something terrible is happening.' said I.

'Hardly, where is the programme? There is probably something on to explain it.'

As Dean said it the screaming and commotion grew closer and louder like a steam train approaching a station. We looked at each other completely forgetting the magnificent creature in the cage before us and listened intently. There was a great crashing noise which bore no explanation by its sound. The great hall filled with so many people and creatures fell into an eerie silence. I was hoping for a great revelation. An intended spectacle that would have us all shout with joy and burst into rapturous applause. Then a woman came running into the great hall.

'*Run, run, run for your lives.*' she screamed.

The woman kept running even when she was inside, holding up her skirt to aid her. I saw people turn their heads deciding whether to run or not; then the huge creature smashed through the front of the Crystal Palace as if it were made of sugar paper.

The giant feathered creature with terrible claws immediately bent down and snapped up a girl in its jaws.

Blood sprayed everywhere from its terrific teeth. The girl fell to the ground in two pieces. It was huge nearly as tall as the palace itself. It had orange feathers with black stripes.

As pandemonium ensued and the crowd started fleeing myself, Dean and Giles all looked at each other and cried in unison '*Elizabeth!*'

It could have only been her for it was the same dinosaur as we had seen on our Hebridean adventure. Besides everybody else involved was too responsible.

People were screaming and being trampled on, priceless artefacts and machines were being carelessly tossed aside and knocked over as they became useless rubbish in the preservation of life.

The beast roared an indescribable sound so loud that some folk even stopped to cover their ears. The creature seemed to enjoy biting folk in half and then discarding them. It tried attacking some prototype agricultural machinery but soon reverted its affections back to humans.

It was getting closer.

'*We can't just run*,' pleaded I. 'We are least partly responsible, we ventured up there and we allowed her to come, God knows how she got one off the island.'

'It is nothing to do with us.' said Dean.

'No, you are correct James we must be men and accept our responsibility. What do you propose?' said Giles.

A large flame erupted from an area adjacent to the entrance. Immediately I knew the great exhibition was over. Then I had an idea, '*The Scotsman*' I yelled.

'What do you mean?' asked Dean.

'Remember he had a huge flaming torch and managed to stop it.'

'Correction, he bought us just enough time to escape.' remarked Giles.

'Confound you, that thing is having a picnic in here we must act now.' said I not hiding my irritation.

'All we are going to do is send it into another crowd.' cried Dean.

'Let us put together a torch.' returned I.

The beast was moving forward. We spotted a nearby display pulled the timber down and getting some fabric fashioned ourselves a torch.

'*We need fuel damn it.*' shouted Giles watching the dinosaur coming ever closer.

'*Oil.*' shouted Dean '*the machines must use oil.*'

We ran to one of the now abandoned stands, looking behind the counter we quickly found several cans of oil we drenched the cloth in it.

'Which one of us should do it?' said I.

'I will.' replied Giles.

'Perhaps it would be fair to flip a coin or throw some dice.' said I not taking my eye off our unexpected intruder.

'No, I should do it. Not only am I the oldest but ultimately it was me who discovered the island in the first place and inadvertently unleashed all of its secrets. Was it not I who coerced you all into joining my adventures?'

'Now, now, we are not counting stock like that.' said I placing my hand on his shoulder.

'It is not a request I am afraid.' he said pulling some matches from his pocket and striking one. I held the oil soaked rag in his direction. The torch ignited with a woof that had us all recoiling, the rancid smell of burning oil filled our nostrils.

'Better scarper gents in case it doesn't work.' said Giles.

'*Never, you may need our help.*' cried I.

'*Well hide then you damn fools.*' returned he.

Myself and Dean did as Giles asked and hid behind some machines that were slightly apart from each other, lest the dreaded beast take us both in one bite. We watched as brave Giles approached it.

'*Listen here beast, go home, go away I tell you, flee, flee.*' shouted Giles.

We had a titter as Dean made a comment regarding a better choice of choice of words. The dinosaur miraculously seemed to listen.

'*Be gone I tell you.*' Giles screamed.

The beast turned around but the fire had gotten out of control, Giles already knew what was to happen next and had already started running when the feathered dinosaur turned and reassessed Giles in an instant. Giles made for an exhibition stand. A large piece of metal was flew through the air and smacked it on the neck.

'*Got it.*' shouted Dean.

'James, what is the matter with you?' said Dean coming over and yanking my arm.

Whilst I was watching it all unfold I was somewhat distracted. Something gnawed at the back of my mind, plagued me, vital information perhaps.

'*We need to go.*' screamed Dean as the dinosaur started heading over to us.

'*Sand.*' I cried. '*It hates sand.*' coming to my senses we both ran through a tunnel hoping to slow the beast down. We saw Giles follow down an adjacent tunnel trying to escape both the bird of terror and the fire.

The giant creature came smashing through after us. We tried to outrun it but were failing fast. As panic was started to materialise into hysteria, the creature suddenly stopped and lost interest. We carried on running into the other section and stopped a minute to gather our senses and rationality.

We saw Giles come out of the other tunnel and upon seeing us started running hither. I recall being surprised at how well he moved for his age; youth was still obviously clinging to him somewhere.

'Sand.' said I 'remember they don't like sand.'

'Yes, I had the same thought as I was running through the tunnel little good it is though.' replied Giles

'What do you mean?' enquired Dean.

'Angus was surrounded by a beach there will be sand in here somewhere but hardly enough to bother it.' said Giles.

'Maybe we should head outside and seek assistance.' said I.

'Yes, that would be wise.' said Dean.

Upon him saying that the dinosaur came smashing through one of the walls.

'Is now a good time?' quipped I.

'*Yes.*' Dean and Giles said in unison. We ran out of one of the numerous exits into the open. Our respiratory tracts were glad of the refreshment.

People were milling about everywhere. We saw an army of Bobbies trying to get through the crowd like ants through long grass. We moved into a quieter area to collect our thoughts.

'We need to find someone in charge; the police commissioner or something.' said I.

'We will have to ask a Bobby.' said Dean.

'It is doubtful anyone that powerful will be on the scene.' remarked Giles.

Suddenly there was a huge explosion as another large section of the Crystal Palace gave way to temptation. There was a collective gasp from the crowd, and to this day it remains one of the eeriest sounds I have ever heard. The fire had become the look of fear and uncertainty filled everybody's eyes.

'*Bessie!*' the single scream came piercing through the subdued crowd like a hunter's bullet into a solitary stag.

We all looked at each other in an instant. It was not the name that got our attention but the voice that screamed it. It was unmistakeable.

'*Elizabeth.*' cried I.

Dean leapt up some crates as agile as a cat. '*She's over there. I see her just past those bushes.*'

I ran around and called her name. She looked startled.

'*They're going to kill Bessie please help me.*'

I grabbed her arm violently. '*Come with me you silly girl.*' I led her back to Giles and Dean.

'*Who is Bessie?*' demanded Giles.

'*It's the confounded dinosaur isn't it?*' I yelled realising my obtuseness.

'Yes.' she replied. At that moment the dinosaur came bursting out of the last section of the palace presumably chased out by the fire. The mighty flames made it look akin to the Phoenix its whole body glowing and twinkling in the firelight, it let out a mighty roar and the crowd screamed in terror.

'*Bessie.*' shouted Elizabeth starting to run off.

Giles grabbed her. 'We need to know everything right now if there is to be any hope of saving both it and you I imagine.'

'Besides it cannot hear you and you have no hope of making it through that crowd.' said I pulling her towards the crates to avoid getting caught in the hysteria.

'*See what you have done you stupid girl.*' shouted Giles '*If your father were still alive he would likely hide you, grown woman or not.*'

Elizabeth looked at the ground.

'*By Jupiter.*' cried Dean.

We looked up and saw a rather portly man in the grips of its terrible teeth. Blood was exploding outwards like lava out of an angry volcano. Shots rang out and the giant bird dropped its snack to the floor with a squelchy thud then it turned to its attackers, we heard a man scream.

The Dinosaur ran off into Hyde Park I saw a group of armed police officers run after it. There was not a soul left in sight apart from a few bloody corpses. The palace was entirely ablaze now never have I seen such a spectacle the heat was immense. You could hear the constant creaking, cracking and popping as wood and metal twisted and writhed.

'Tell me everything now please.' Giles said firmly.
'What here?' replied Elizabeth.
'Why not?' replied I sitting on one of the crates and secretly starting to enjoy the great fire that accompanied us.
'Ok.' she replied with a sigh. It was then that Elizabeth explained how when she had stayed behind in the room she had procured one of the hatchlings, and how after successfully unfastening the lock she had carried it in her big leather bag the whole time. Also how she fed her father a load of bunkum about needing an ever bigger place for experimentation and study. Which he was only too glad to provide as she was following him into science.

She confided in us how it became her pet and as she was its sole source of food and company it never so much as looked at her the wrong way. After discovering the lock broken all she had to was follow the trail of destruction.

'*Didn't you realise?* Why do you think when we stopped in Edinburgh on the way home I was ordering all that food. It was to keep my darling Bessie alive.' Elizabeth blurted finishing her narrative.

'Why did you call it Bessie?' asked Dean.
'It was my father's pet name for me as a little girl.' she replied twiddling her hair as if it somehow transported her back there. I remember failing to imagine her as ever being sweet.

'How very apt.' chuckled I.
Giles gave a loud guffaw at this. Dean smiled whilst Elizabeth remained stoical as if not getting the joke.

We heard screams and saw the dinosaur run out of the park and down Albert's Road.

'I hope you are right Elizabeth and you can control this thing. You are the only hope we have.'

'Come on.' said I leading the charge. We ran out onto Kensington Road.

There was a line of cabs awaiting fares as if nothing had happened. I admired their bravery yet they weren't alone.

People had started to gather to watch the greatest fire since 1666. We all jumped into a clarence and raced down Queen's Gate, we could see the dinosaur way ahead. By the time we were halfway down the road it was long out of view. We eventually made it to the junction with Cromwell road and saw the dinosaur was outside the Brompton Park House (which would later become the Victoria and Albert Museum) on the corner of Exhibition Road.

The driver turned onto Cromwell road but refused to get too close. We jumped out about halfway and saw the dinosaur heading back towards us. People were screaming and running there was also more bodies. As it came towards us a couple of soldiers appeared and took shots at it with rifles; it bit one of them in half where he stood. We watched in a terrorised stupor as his legs remained standing on their own, I nearly vomited.

Elizabeth was not discouraged and ran toward it. '*Elizabeth.*' we cried snapping out of our stupor. The bird continued unabated and went after the other soldier soon he was nothing but an interesting pattern on the floor.

Elizabeth ran forward just as a garrison arrived. They immediately aimed Elizabeth's beloved Bessie.

'*No, no!*' Elizabeth screamed. She spied the gun on the floor, kicked over the standing legs of the soldier who had been bitten in half and picked up his gun. She ran towards her beloved bird. The dinosaur was being pummelled by bullets and at last we could start to see blood appearing through its feathers. It was about to run but upon seeing Elizabeth it changed its mind and turned to attack the garrison but as it did another garrison appeared some of which were now firing the new so called 'Elephant Gun'.

The terrible lizard let out a blood-curdling scream which still haunts me to this day.

'*Nooooooooooo!*' Elizabeth screamed as she started firing at the soldiers. The first shot hit one of them square in the shoulder. Approaching her beloved dinosaur she tried to take another shot but instead received a volley of bullets into her chest. Blood seeped through her clothing as if she were an inkblot. A brief look of surprise then she dropped to the floor. With a mighty crash seconds later her beloved pet did the same. The guns went silent, and there was not a sound to be heard as if the whole of London had gone into mourning.

We stood there trying to take it all in. Then we witnessed a most remarkable event. Elizabeth bleeding profusely pulled herself over to Bessie using her bloodied hands. Right up to its face she went; the bird reciprocated by lifting its giant head as if to nuzzle her. She kissed it on the cheek and laid her face against it then they died together against the backdrop of a winter sunset caused by the mighty palace fire.

As bizarre as it may seem I have never seen such a moving moment as that. Behind locked doors it visits me often as if to plague me of some hidden doubt, a regret through my inaction, through my many disparaging thoughts about Elizabeth. In the end, she had dared to sacrifice her life for the greatest bird that ever lived. It is now I will close my narrative for I wish to think on it no more.

The only two things left of interest is that someone who witnessed the event took inspiration and that is how it became the site for the Natural History Museum.

In addition, the broadsheets the next day carried no story - no fire, no dinosaur, nothing. One or two of the major ones carried a story about the Crystal Palace being moved for logistical purposes; Sydenham I think is the place that they mentioned.

Such Fun

'Excuse me sir I wish to donate to you on this drizzled afternoon, would you mind if I took some change though as I only have crowns.

'Not all thank you for your generosity.'

The man leant forward and as he did he flicked his hand toward the beggar's haggard face. No reaction not even a flinch. He dropped in some three-penny bits, as loud as he could, then slyly retrieved three sovereigns from the cup.

'There you go that should help you through.' the man chirped.

'God bless ya sir.' said the beggar doffing a dirty blue cap.

'You are most welcome.' the man replied cracking a smile.

The fragrance of fresh manure filled the air. Normally he found the smell repulsive but on this particular occasion he quite liked it.

'Afternoon.' he said lifting his bowler hat.

'Afternoon.' the wealthy couple replied with the man tipping his top hat in response.

He strolled onto the pebbled street that contained his small terraced house without compunction thinking his devious thoughts and plotting his nefarious schemes.

The man whistled to himself, the smell of fresh manure dissipating somewhat as he left the main street, the beginnings of an autumnal evening were trying to work their way into the sky.

He approached his white door and scraped his foot on the iron grating; he stepped inside and took off his boots. The acrid stench of gas lighting welcomed him home like a dog that always bites. The sweet aroma of his wife's cooking finally reached his nostrils.

'How was your day darling?'

'It was splendid darling. I met a blind man on my way home, his tin cup was nearly full, I could hardly fathom it once I saw he had three sovereigns in there.'

'That is surprising, lucky man.'

'No my dear lucky *us*. I had the fortune to have plenty of small change so I wished him well and put in three penny bits, and unfortunately these happened to come back out with my hand.' the man beamed a mischievous smile before revealing three shiny gold sovereigns in his palm.

'Oh you are wicked.' his wife said laughing.

'He doesn't need all that money: he has enough for rum. I told you I would provide for you didn't I?'

'You did that's why I married you Ryan Stagsden.'

'And I am the better off for it Mrs Isabel Stagsden. Anyway that beggar is evil he probably did something wrong in a past life.'

'Ha, I'm sure he did.' chuckled his wife.

'Do you fancy taking the little one on a trip to the zoo on the morrow?'

'What a fabulous idea.'

'After all we have the money.' Ryan smiled a fiendish grin yet again and looked at his wife. She smiled back flicking her black hair in a coquettish manner.

The aroma of gravy and meat filled the room as Isabel served up dinner.

'What are we having tonight dear?'

'We are having Beef, Cauliflower and boiled potatoes with gravy.'

'Thank you Isabel you are a wonderful cook, and how is our little boy?'

'He is fine, asleep upstairs I checked just before you got home.'

'So come on how was work today? You have not given the slightest of inclinations.'

'Yes I have.' said Ryan reaching for his mug of beer to wash the food down. 'You have been informed that I had a good day haven't you?'

'That maybe but you have not stopped grinning since you got home, I know you there is something you have not divulged.'

Ryan looked up at his wife whilst cutting off a sliver off beef to wrap around a potato. 'You know me too well.'

'I am your wife, Queen Victoria sits on the throne, it startles me that men are still surprised by our intuition.'

'Well I never quite said that Isabel.' Ryan said rolling up his sleeves and looking away with a miffed expression on his face. 'Do you remember I told you that there was little chance of me progressing because Harold was next in line for promotion at work?'

There was a silence while his wife finished a mouthful of food; she gently dabbed her mouth with a handkerchief then spoke. 'Yes I remember.'

'As it happens he has had to finish work slightly earlier than usual giving me the opportunity to work with Cedric directly.'

'The owner?'

'Yes, the highest himself. Hitherto he had always kept me at a distance but I saw my chance to strike once he started engaging in conversation with me. Previously Harold had informed of the personal goings on with him. This meant that I was aware he had lost a son to the pox before I had started.

I mentioned to him that perhaps Harold was not the man that he surmised him to be. Casually I suggested that he might be a slanderer and a rumour spreader. When he asked me why, I informed Cedric that Harold had told me about him losing his son to the pox and that he only caught it because he does not look after his family well enough. You should have seen his face.' Ryan burst out laughing as he shoved a fork full of vegetables into his mouth still laughing as he started to chew.

'Did he ejaculate violently?'

'To fathom how he didn't is beyond my comprehension for he obviously believed every word. I quickly reassured him that of course I did not believe a single word of it and was steadfast in my conviction that he was a fine father and that he was a fiend for making up lies about him losing a child.

I remember he took a deep breath to calm himself down, then he informed me solemnly that he did lose a child, but there was nothing that could have been done and it was certainly not his fault.'

'So what about when he asks Harold about it?'

'Really my dear do you doubt my cunning, albeit I will admit there was some luck in it, for it was Cedric himself that made me think of that eventuality when he remarked how cowardly Harold was for not saying it to his face.

Immediately I acted as fearful as I possibly could and said that Harold had threatened to kill me if I ever told him what I had said. He reassured me of his protection but I was not convinced that he had fully bought my story.

There was no alternative; I broke down to almost a whimper imploring him not to. I informed Cedric that he was blissfully unaware of the violent outbursts that occurred when he was not in the office and that I often dreaded the moment he departed for the day. Trying to convince him thoroughly I told him that Harold had slapped me once when I stood my ground to him. Cedric looked horrified. I quickly explained that the only reason Harold has not struck me since is because I threatened to report it. The reprisal from Harold would be unthinkable that's why he must not know.

Cedric turned away from me, I saw a look of doubt cross his face, I had gone too far I knew I had.

Look, I do suppose that he is acting like a bad fellow but with all the stress of his wife being ill sometimes people change. He used to be a hard worker now he makes me do his as well as mine, you can see for yourself, it is all signed off by myself. Harold is not the same man I started working for.

Apologies Cedric I should not have said anything I will return to my work and never make mention of it.

From then on it was all too easy. I was often called into his office, he wanted me to spend time with him do special projects and all the time Harold was being left out more and more. I tell you darling it was so funny watching him struggle to work out what was going on. He knew something was amiss he even tried to ask Cedric what the problem was but he would not tell him. I had to stop myself from smiling.

Every time his name came up or Harold popped into have a word I would wait until he was gone and then just say something subtle like 'there's something not right about him these days.' Not too much lest Cedric get suspicious but just enough to keep the seed watered and growing.

'So did he really make you do all his work?'

'Ha.' Ryan replied with a loud guffaw. 'Not at all, in fact quite the opposite. When his wife became ill and he started leaving early I saw the chance to start taking over. I offered him my condolences and insisted that he allow me take on some of his workload.

The idea was to learn his job so I could take it from him but I quickly realised the advantages of signing his work off. I took on some of his work load yes, but what I also started doing was finishing his work off right at the end of each project. That way he did all the work but I signed them off, and for the past week nearly everything that has gone to Cedric has been signed off by me.

I was in disbelief when I realised how advantageous this had become in his office the other night. As soon as I mentioned to him about me doing all the work he looked down at the pile of documents all signed by me and nodded his agreeableness.

That, my dear, brings us to today. Sensing that it was really affecting Harold I stopped helping him the last couple of days feigning an extra project I had been given. Harold's output was now minimal and his mistakes many. Cedric called him upstairs and fired him. It was almost as delicious as this beef I tell you. There was a heated exchange and Cedric came charging down the stairs and threw the front door open ordering him out. He then started *crying.*'

'*Crying*, a man at work, really?'

'Yes, I could not believe it, he was babbling on about he did not know what had gone wrong and his work had only dropped because of that. Of course, it was all true which to me made it all the funnier. Then he launched a scathing attack at me calling me names and saying he knew it was all me; it was perfect. I was so glad that I said he had threatened to kill me because he was now playing straight into my hands as it were. I leapt up from the desk, put the most frightened expression that I could on my face, then I clapped my hands together as if praying and shouted in a desperate plea as if I was in fear for my life. '*I swear to God it was nothing to do with me; please Harold please don't hurt me.'*

You should have seen his face, it was agog with surprise, a blanket of bewilderment and perplexity.

Cedric who as you recall is not a particularly small man grabbed Harold by the collar and threatened that if he ever touched me or came after me he would see to it that he would come off worse.

Not knowing what to do I decided to remain looking frightened and rather shaken. Cedric turned to me and apologised, told me not to worry, then informed me that I had been promoted to Harold's role and that he was even going to pay me a bit more. In reply I thanked him and said I would immediately start sorting the work load out and preparing for the extra duties. I also informed him that I would be staying late to get everything as organised as possible. He replied that was nonsense and that I should take a large glass of Brandy to settle my nerves and to ensure that Harold had cleared the area then I should take rest of the afternoon off.'

His wife had finished eating and rather demurely she laid the cutlery on the plate.

'You're wicked.' she said.

'He's evil.'

'You say everyone is evil.'

'Only those who are in my way.' replied Ryan purposefully covering his mouth like a child who had let some big secret slip.

He and his wife both laughed.

'Anyway it was such fun.' a huge nefarious grin crossed his face as he put his last mouthful of food in.

'So you have been promoted and received a large pay rise?'

'Yes my dear; we have much cause for celebration.'

Having slept well Ryan was in a jubilant mood that usually meant he would be crueler than ever, but only to those who either do not realise or are in no position to fight back.

Ryan dressed as if it were a workday in shirt, trousers and shoes. Then he added a waistcoat and a pocket watch with a chain across the pockets. Looking at his voluminous hair he smiled to himself thinking that he that he would be of a great age before balding ever set in. Finally he went downstairs to see how his wife was getting on.

She was just putting their daughter into the perambulator. His wife was wearing a long green dress with a bustle at the back and a matching bonnet. He smiled warmly at her and then opened the door so they could set off for the zoo.

'I think we should walk to the zoo dear don't you? After all the sun is warm and the air is fresh.'

'Yes I agree, the underground is so smoky and loud, I dread to think what it does to our little one.'

They walked to the zoo without incident and just one of the sovereigns gained them entrance.

The first place they visited in the huge zoo was a menagerie of livestock that the public could interact with.

'Look darling there is a horse.' he said to his son. Ryan leant down and took an apple out of his wife's bag. 'Watch this.' he said approaching the fence holding out the apple. A horse quickly saw it and gaily trotted toward its golden prize.

'Do you want this apple? Come on ... take it ... take it.'

The horse eagerly put its head through the fence to take the apple just as it furled up its lips and began to bring down its teeth; Ryan snatched it away and took a bite himself.

'Well you can't have it, it's mine, *it's all mine.*' he said laughing as bits of juice and apple sprayed everywhere.

'Isn't your daddy cruel eh?' his wife said.

The man turned around being careful not to muddy his shoes. 'You know what darling you are correct as ever; I will stop being so cruel. There you go Mr Horsey have your apple.' he said putting it on the grass just outside the fence. The horse immediately put his head through to get it, but it was just out of reach. The horse tried in vain to squeeze its head through but it couldn't, and then it got its head stuck. It brayed violently and kicked up its back legs until suddenly it was free again. The horse stood there looking at the apple trying to figure out how to get it.

The man stood there laughing, his wife chuckled.

'*Don't look at me Isabel* it is there if he wants it.'

'A zoo keeper is coming.' urged his wife.

Ryan's face changed. 'Come on let's start walking.'

They walked away from the horses in the direction of the zookeeper. Ryan wondered whether he had been spotted teasing the horse.

'Good morning folks.' the keeper said doffing his black cap.

'Good morning to you sir.' Replied Ryan

'Are you enjoying the zoo?'

'It's simply wonderful.' said his wife.

'Yes I was just saying that to you wasn't I dear. I adore the animals it is such a pleasure to visit I am even thinking of donating to you.'

'Jolly good sir, you know there is nothing like meeting a fellow animal lover.'

'If I can be of assistance I will.' replied Ryan flashing a friendly smile.

'Alas I must continue my rounds but it was good to meet you, hopefully I will see you again.'

With that the two parties walked their separate ways. The man's wife gently nudged him in ribs. '*You are such a liar.*'

'He doesn't know that does he? Besides I really do love coming here. Where shall we go next.' he said rubbing his hands with glee.

So the day continued. When he visited the geese and ducks, he would attract them to him with food then boot them up the behind, sometime's he would lift them up with his foot and send them flying through air. He spat in a llama's face before it knew what was going on.

Just as they started to consider luncheon they entered the primate section.

'Of course how could I forget that stupid ape?'

'Don't lie to me I'm sure you only come here to tease it every time we visit we spend twenty minutes in it's company and by that I mean it screeching and jumping around the cage in anger at you.'

'Ok, my sweet wife ten minutes max I promise. Look, that ape has its back to us.' Ryan held his finger over his mouth to indicate for his wife to be silent. Their baby son had already fallen asleep. He crept silently up to the cage and then shouted and banged on the bars; the ape leapt high into the air and danced around the cage screaming and swinging from its branches. Yet again Ryan burst out laughing until he noticed another ape in the cage that was sat with his back to him. It was looking out of the bars at the other end, and it was very young.

'What have we here, you're a brave one aren't you?' he said running around the other side of the cage and banging on the bars violently. The young primate screamed in terror and ran straight to the older ape then jumped into its arms.

'This is such fun. Now where is the ape I normally come to visit?'

'I don't know ... oh look there he is, in that cage over there, he is watching you.' replied his wife pointing.

Ryan looked up and saw the ape that he particularly enjoyed taunting sitting in a new cage staring at him. The man went to his wife's bag and pulled out a banana. It was starting to go brown and the skin felt rubbery in his hands.

'Come on dear. He can stare all he wants but I am still going to have some fun with him.'

His wife giggled as she pushed the perambulator behind him.

The ape as if expecting him folded its arms tightly as he approached the cage.

'Would you like a banana? Look they're delicious.' he said slowly unpeeling it and wafting it in front of his own nose. He offered it to the ape but it looked away from him.

'I think it has learned to ignore you.' said Isabel laughing.

'It won't be able to resist; you watch.' said the man leaning in through the bars to taunt the ape. The ape held his composure and refused to look.

'I think we have a tough guy here.' said Ryan looking at his wife with a mischievous grin on his face. 'Don't worry I will scare him instead then.'

As he looked back the ape lunged forward and grabbed his shirt; Ryan's head slammed into the bars. The ape pulled his face right up to it. Ryan tried not to gag as the overwhelming stench of rotting vegetables from the primate's breath filled his nostrils.

The ape looked him straight in the eye staring at him with incredible intensity. At first, he was not sure what was going on as Ryan suddenly found himself looking back at himself. He thought someone must have suddenly slid a mirror between them. Then he noticed his hands were hairy and they were holding his own shirt, they were different, they were the hands of an ape. He released his grip then stared down at himself and saw the body of an ape.

'*No ... no it can't be ... it can't be it is impossible ... impossible I tell you.*' Ryan cried. He fell back in shock as he heard the sound of his own voice was nothing but the squawks and screams of an ape. Sheer panic consumed him, he jumped around the cage banging and screaming with terror and hysteria, the fierce energy of desperation surging through his veins.

A huge burly zookeeper with a notorious reputation for cruelty entered the cage from a back door.

'*I'll give you something to scream about you stupid monkey.*'

Ryan leapt back to the front of the cage and saw the physical form of himself sidle up to his wife with an over affectionate cuddle. The simian-man, looking back at him, smiled as he put his arm around her waist and said:

'You know what; *this is* going to be such fun!'

As the couple walked off the only sound was of wood meeting simian flesh.

The Box

'Gone, gone it's gone I tell you, I cannot find the confounded thing anywhere.'

'Calm down sir. Please I beg of you, what is gone?'
'The box. My box.'
'It is here somewhere I assure you.'
'Don't get bloody-minded with me my good man, you take me for an imbecile, I know damn well where I left it.'

'Where did you leave it?'
'Right here blast you, where do you think?'
'And you're absolutely sure?'
'Sure enough to box you square on the nose if you ask me that again.'
'I must ask these questions it is my duty.'
'Your duty? Your duty is to protect my valuables, yet you haven't. Now your duty is to get them back, you ...' the man lunged forward and grabbed the station attendant by the lapels of his jacket, *'why you ...'*

The other man looked visibly shaken. A man in a brown bowler hat sitting on a nearby bench jumped up and pushed his way between the two.

'Calm down, the man is just trying to do his job, what is the problem?'

The aggressor's complexion changed to a brief look of shame. 'My box ... it's gone.'

'What was in it?'

'Treasure.'

'Treasure, what was its value?' asked the intervening man.

'Damn you man it was priceless.'

A couple of unsavoury looking men on a nearby bench looked at each other.

'When did you see it last?' the man said continuing his line of questioning.

'I left to get a ticket that is all. The station attendant was guarding the luggage section; what did I have to fear?'

The newcomer looked to the station attendant for an answer.

'I had a customer to see to. I was not gone but two minutes.'

'Ere, mister.' said an unshaven gentleman in a flat cap, he was one of the two that had been eavesdropping on the conversation.'

'Yes.' returned he who had lost his property.

'If we help you get your box will there be a reward?'

The man's face lit up like the moon on a clear night. '*By Jove yes*. You will all be rewarded.'

'And there is priceless treasure inside?' asked the station attendant.

'*Absolutely.*' the man replied.

'*You* have to stay near the station.' sneered the man in the flat cap pointing at the attendant.

'Not if there is a reward in it I do not.' replied the station attendant throwing his hat into the luggage. 'Now how do we find the dastardly villains?'

The man in the flat cap whistled to his confederate who promptly joined them.

Without introduction he spoke. 'I saw some weird looking geezer inspecting the luggage and upon seeing your box took fancy to it he did. He picked it up and carried it out as if it were his own, of course me being familiar with such roguish characters immediately knew what he was up to, but it weren't none of my business was it? Well, not up until now anyways.' the man flashed a mischievous grin which displayed his bright yellow teeth.

'Well, where did he go and what did he look like man?'

'He had scraggly blonde looking hair underneath a black hat not dissimilar to mine you see.'

'And how do we find him?' said the stranger who had intervened in the first instance.

'Simple, follow me.' said the man in the flat cap.

'Halt.' said the station attendant in an authoritative tone. 'Surely we should know each other's names from this point on – my name is Bill.' he said pointing to his name badge.

'And I, the cause of this trouble, am Gordon.'

'I am Arthur.' said the man who broke up the fight.

'And I am Wayne and my friend ere is Marcus.'

It was Marcus who had witnessed the event and who was keen to lead the party outside.

Gordon surveyed his willful helpers. Bill was a station attendant clearly and not much more was to be said about him. Arthur seemed to be a wealthy and confident gentleman, surely a concerned citizen. Gordon watched as Arthur retrieved Bill's station hat from the luggage and placed it back on his head.

With Wayne and Marcus there was something off in their demeanour, in the way they acted, the way they behaved and Marcus had a crooked nose that spoke of violence. Gordon's gut quivered like a string on a violin.

They had a nefarious way about them, but considering his precious box was already missing what did he have to lose?

'Come outside quickly if you want to see your treasure again.' Marcus barked as if he was reading Gordon thoughts.

The party did not hesitate and were glad to be rid of the steam and smoke of the station. Outside was a row of hansoms, people were milling everywhere and the aroma of fresh manure had replaced the stench of acrid smoke. The evening was pleasant but fog was starting to appear and outer garments could now be witnessed.

'What now?' Gordon cried.

'Trust us.' said Wayne flashing a smile that revealed one black tooth. He nudged Marcus in the ribs.

'Like I said a man looking that unusual cannot be that hard to trace.' said Marcus.

'But how?' asked Arthur.

'I can ask the staff.' quipped Bill.

Marcus rolled his eyes and pulled straight his worn-out brown suit. He then approached the first hansom in the line with Wayne in tow and spoke to the driver. The others watched as the driver lifted his top hat and began conversing with Marcus.

'The cab would have gone way before now if the perpetrator had taken one.' reasoned Bill.

'Yes, that is true.' added Arthur. 'Might I have a word in private, Gordon?'

They both looked at Bill who shrugged his shoulders and stepped back. Arthur pulled Gordon close to him. 'I have to tell you my dear fellow, I trust neither Wayne nor Marcus. They could even be part of it.'

'In cahoots?' replied Arthur.

'Yes and keep your voice down. There is something not right about them two, I am telling you.'

'I admit I have some reservations.'

'There we go we should act.'

'How? It doesn't make sense; why should he help us? Why should he even approach? They could have been well away by now if they had taken it.'

'You have a point but I trust my instinct.'

Bill wandered back over.

'We should not stand about we have no hope of recovering my box if we do not set about it immediately.' snapped Gordon.

'Here he comes.' said Arthur watching as Marcus approached collecting Wayne en route.

'Right fellas, I have the skinny on im. He caught a hansom all we have to do is wait for him to return.'

'Explain.' said bill.

Marcus sneered briefly. 'The cab was obviously not the one he took but the driver knows who did and being an unmistakeable client he has no doubt that it was our man who took the cab.'

'Outstanding.' replied Gordon clapping his hands.

'How will we know what driver is the correct one?' said Bill.

'We will have to ask everyone I suppose.' said Gordon kicking a loose stone out of his quarter.

'No such thing sir, he was a mottled horse you see.' said Marcus with a grin.

'And how many mottled horses do you see in London pulling cabs? They're all shiny black or brown.' Wayne said joining in for the sake of it.

'Or ostentatious white.' Arthur added.

'Yes quite.' said Bill adjusting his hat.

Gordon studied the face of Marcus and Wayne he realised their mischievous look was not necessarily a sign of stupidity.

'Well done, excellent, you have everything covered by the sounds of it.' Gordon said raising his voice higher than intended.

'Indeed we do sir.' replied Wayne.

'Marcus and Wayne at your service.' replied Marcus taking a bow.

Gordon withheld a shudder. The party stood there watching the hansom's return one at a time and with every minute Gordon grew more anxious.

Just as Arthur was about to step forward and console his visibly distressed companion a cab pulled by a mottled horse came into the station. The party ran over like a pack of rabid dogs after a lame fox.

'*Sir, sir, my good sir, help us please.*' cried Gordon in a pant of desperation.

'Ere allow me.' said Marcus pushing his way through. 'We happen to know that you just carried a fare out of this ere place with stolen goods you see.'

'Look my good sir, we know you have nothing to do with it but my good friend has had precious cargo stolen from him, you can see for yourself, we are with the station porter.' said Arthur pushing his way to the front.

Bill straightened his Jacket. 'It is true my good man.' he said deepening his voice.

'Tell us what we need to know.' said Wayne.

'What do you need to know?' replied the cabbie stroking his silver handlebar moustache.

'Where did you take him?' said Wayne

'Exactly where?' said Marcus interjecting.

'But we can't all fit in the hansom we need a clarence.' cried Bill.

'Then we shall take two. Whatever the coin is I shall pay it.' said Gordon flicking his hand in dismissal.

'Did you get his name?' Arthur asked.

'Out of politeness I asked but all I got was called nosey, but with a most obscene vulgarity might I add.'

'Gentleman please we can talk on the way.' said Gordon motioning them to their respective cabs.

The cabs shook violently as they forced themselves along the cobbles, yet all of them sat in harmony with the violent rhythm as if they were the creators of it.

'Where are we headed?' shouted Arthur.

'The Nichol.' replied the driver nonchalantly.

'*The Nichol.*' shrieked Bill with a cry of despair.

'Take heart, we are many in number.' said Gordon.

After fifteen minutes they pulled up. 'He went down that there alley and that is all I can tell you I promise.' said the Cab driver.

Gordon, Arthur and Bill heard the other hansom pull up behind them and with invigorated confidence Gordon leapt out of the hansom like a soldier onto a fresh battlefield. All of them followed Gordon's lead as he ran into the maze of dark alleyways.

The Nichol - a place that God himself avoided. A rabbit warren of destitution and poverty, rancid smells made you wretch and despair crept upon your hopes. Despite being early evening the Nichol had its own ecosystem – midnight already; dark and gloomy reeking with desolation like a house marked with the plague.

They saw a group of young teenagers wearing flat caps. Before any of the group could scarper Marcus ran forward and lifted one of the lads high against the wall. There was a loud slap as his back hit the brickwork.

'Listen ere young lad, if you don't want me to open you up so all your friends can see you inside out you will tell me exactly what I need to know. A man with blond locks and a top hat came running through ere a short while ago, who was he and where did he go? And don't tell me that he

didn't come through ere or I'll test me new knife on ya.'
Marcus brandished a large steel blade from about his person.

The boy in the flat cap gulped and dropped the wooden club that he had surreptitiously produced from his back pocket. Marcus was not phased, he stared at the young boy like a cobra.

'Yeah he lives ere mister. I seen him plenty of times before you see.'

'Where'd he go?' snapped Gordon lunging forward.

'You promise - *we never told you a word.*' the vagabond pleaded purposefully including his cohorts.

'You have our word.' said Arthur boldly stepping forward as if he were a headmaster addressing a school.

'Ok mister, I saw him alright he went in that there door. Mean fella he is, always thieving, never cares about anyone.' said the boy looking as if he had just given his own confessional.

'Right.' said Gordon.

'I think he is linked to one of these ere gangs. The doctors ... nurses ...'

'*The Medics?*' shrieked Marcus.

'Yeah that's them.' the urchin replied wiping his hands on his coat.

'I've heard of them.' said Bill.

'He's not a member though at least not that I know of.'

'Go on.' urged Gordon.

'I heard they shake him down regular you see, he likes to hit the train stations and the medics say that's their turf, so he has to pay em. Not that he's that bothered from what I can tell. He comes home with something new every night, well new to him anyhow.' the boy laughed heartily and put on his cap.

'Ok we get it, and you're sure he went in that door there.' said Gordon pointing to a door a small ways down the alley.

'I swear to it sir.'

Gordon pulled out a half-crown and flipped it to him.

'Don't give him money.' Marcus protested.

'Why not we have inconvenienced him haven't we?'

'You're a good man.' said Arthur placing his hand on Gordon's shoulder.

'Thank you sir if you need anything else just ask.' the urchin replied.

Gordon laughed. 'Here share this with your friends.' he said flipping the street urchin a whole crown.

'*Geez mister thanks*, listen there's more than one way out of them there rooms, I can tell you, I have seen him make a run for it when the medics have come calling before.'

'Excellent you have earnt your pay and I expect you and your friends to keep out of trouble tonight, you have earnt enough for now I'm sure.'

'Gladly mister, come back here anytime you need to know about the Nichol.'

'Indeed I will son now off you go.'

The young lad ran off.

'*Idiot*.' Wayne snapped looking at Gordon.

'I am not sure that was wise now everybody in this God forsaken place will know that you have money.' added Bill.

'Maybe Bill should lead this party from now on.' said Marcus.

'Yeah, if you want our help stop taking the lead and acting like a bleedin idiot.' Wayne said leaning in a little too close for comfort.

'Hang on a minute gentleman, there are five of us and so far no one has been shy, besides he got the information out of him did he not?' said Arthur.

'Yes I did and I would thank you to remember that it is *my* box that is missing and that it is *my* quarry you are seeking – if you want a reward that is.' replied Gordon.

Wayne backed off. 'Yeah well, I tend to gets carried away you see; especially when you put our lives in danger.'

'Nonsense, I gave us the edge now let us not lose the advantage. I suggest we listen at the door as we knock that way we can hear if anyone hurriedly clears out.' before anyone could answer Gordon strolled toward the door.

'*Ere,* steady on fella.' urged Marcus putting his hand in his jacket for a weapon.

'What are we going to say?' said Bill.

'Never considered that.' replied Gordon standing on the few concrete steps leading up to the front door.

'We have to use Bill he's the one in uniform.' replied Arthur running his finger around the rim his bowler hat.

'How? What can *I* say?'

'Listen, all we need is for em to open the door. Say you believe he may have dropped something valuable in the station.' said Marcus.

'So how do we know where he lives?' remarked Gordon.

'Good point that is.' said Wayne rubbing his chin.

'Let's hope he isn't that clever is what I say.' said Arthur in exasperation.

'Oh hell there's five of us let's try anything.' said Marcus pulling something out of his hair.

Bill gulped but remained silent. Before anyone could pronounce a verdict Wayne hammered on the door.

'*Who the bleedin ell is that*?' shrieked a woman's voice.

Gordon turned around and grabbed Bill by his uniform and yanked him violently forward.

'Uh ... my name is Bill I am a station porter at *Kings Cross* Station. I believe you may have dropped something valuable.

Arthur and Gordon had their ears pressed hard against the door whilst Wayne and Marcus had their heads over each of Bill's shoulder's making him feel claustrophobic.

'Who is it?' a male voice demanded.

'*I dunno some porter from the station.*' came the woman's reply.

'He must have brought the peelers, don't answer it, tell em you're aving a bath or something.'

'*They've rumbled us.*' said Arthur pulling his ear away from the door.

'We heard.' replied Wayne.

'We have to act now or all is lost.' said Gordon desperately.

Marcus kicked down the door with one solid hard kick. Bill gasped at the sudden violence. A woman in undergarments screamed as they all piled in. Immediately they saw the man with blonde locks was going through a back door with the box in his hand.

Arthur took the lead. There was paper and trash scattered everywhere. He ran and leapt over a small coffee table when a woman in a filthy dress came running out of the connecting corridor holding up a large knife. She screamed like a mother watching her child die. Arthur punched her full bore in the face. She flew back as if she had been hit by a train and landed with an unconscious thud. Arthur made the sign of the cross and moved on, then that the shot rang out.

'*Good God. He is firing on us.*' cried Gordon hugging the side of the corridor.

'It's ok I'm carrying.' said Arthur pulling out a revolver.

Wayne and Marcus looked at each other with surprise.

Arthur charged ahead ready to let off a shot, but the assailant had vanished. He charged through a door with such force that it mattered not whether it was locked. Another small room that looked akin to Aladdin's cave with various trinkets and discarded stolen goods strewn across the table and floor. The sole of their quarry's foot was all they managed to glimpse as he jumped out of the window.

Arthur ran forward and found he had a clean shot on their fleeing suspect. One shot in the centre of the back would put him down and ensure that he would not get up, but that would not do he was just a thief, not *the ripper*.

'*Get after im.*' cried Wayne.

Arthur leapt out of the window as if he were the one being pursued. Another shot into the brickwork right by his head; this time he returned fire with no compunction. The sound of the gunshot bounced around the Nichol like a wasp caught in a glass. Within seconds the entire party was outside.

'*Confound you sir, we will apprehend you*!' cried Gordon.

Wayne and Marcus both had their knives out ready to strike. The man they were seeking was standing around the corner waiting for them and he had three other men with him all with their sleeves rolled up.

Arthur instinctively put his gun away and Wayne and Marcus sheathed their weapons but ensuring that they were still easily accessible.

Like a bee making its honeypot next to a bear's cave the audacious villain had laid out the box on a concrete step behind them. The man with the crazy blonde hair stood there beckoning them to enter into a duel with them. His three compatriots were of reasonable build and seemed to be no stranger to violence. They bore the scars of a thousand skirmishes.

The standoff lasted about thirty seconds. Gordon rushed forward screaming with anger, the thief did not cower but ran forward to greet him and although Gordon landed a successful punch, it was quickly returned. A brawl ensued with everyone landing successful punches but getting blessed in return. As heads rolled, eyes blackened and noses bled it was Bill that surprised everyone. Marcus, Wayne, Arthur and Gordon himself all supposed that he would wither, spectate or ambulate as fast he could in the other direction, but rage consumed him and it was Bill that turned the tables with several well-aimed punches.

One man received a direct punch on the nose but not content with that bill had followed up with an impressive uppercut and laid the man to waste. The war was coming to an end but the blonde perpetrator saw what was to come and in the fracas grabbed the box off of the step. He smashed through the red front door.

Panicking Arthur pulled out his gun and Marcus and Wayne pulled out their knives. The pack of warriors became poppies in an orchard.

'*We was just lookin out for our mate that's all.*' cried the one with a shaved head.

'*Yeah what's this all about anyways?*' said another laying his hands out in gesture.

'Just get out of here – *now* – and do not let me see you again.' said Arthur pulling the hammer noisily back on his gun and pointing it at the ginger one.

'Yes sir, no fear of that.'

With that the men got up and walked off, Gordon noticed a sly grin on one of their faces.

'They were just slowing us down.' said Gordon with a sigh.

'Yeah well, this better be bleedin worth it.' Marcus said with blood seeping from a cut on his cheek.

'Let us not waste time arguing about it we have to continue after the fiend.' said Arthur.

Through the shattered door they found a family with terror-filled eyes.

'*Which way did he go?*' shouted Bill with such assertion the others had to double check that it was Bill who shouted it.

'*Through there.*' the small man replied pointing through an open window.

One by one like horses over a furlough the pursuant party piled into yet another alley, but saw their perpetrator in a fistfight with a giant of a man.

'*My box*!' yelled Gordon seeing it lying on the floor.

A mighty thump sent their quarry flying to the ground. The huge man was over six feet tall with a thickset moustache and a baldhead. He looked at the newcomers as if not sure whether he was to take them on as well.

'Thank you kind stranger.' said Arthur before anyone could speak. 'We have chased this villain all across east London.'

'Well I heard my neighbour cry out and saw this man climbing from the window, he will think twice about coming it strange around my patch again'

'Indeed he will.' laughed Gordon with a song in his voice.

'We can take it from here my good sir thank you for your assistance.' said Arthur stepping forward and offering his hand.

The man in his dirty vest accepted the invitation, shook his hand firmly and disappeared back into his house.

Gordon already had the box in his hand.

'*Have the stupid bloody thing.*' cursed the blonde man on the ground. He looked like a tomato that had been used in a game of squash.

'Gentleman I cannot thank you enough you have restored my very life to me and in reward we shall be going to the finest restaurant, you can all feast like kings at my expense.'

'*Feast like Kings*, your avin us on aren't you?' said Wayne stepping to him.

'Yeah we want what's in this box.' said Wayne marching forward and snatching the box from him.

'*How dare you*? *You rogue.*' protested Gordon as Wayne opened the box.

'*What – this is it – this is your treasure this ... this ... this!*' screamed Wayne like a wounded animal. '*We did all that for just for this.*' he said pulling out some brown photographs and worthless memorabilia.

Arthur burst into a hearty guffaw that turned to raucous laughter. Bill seeing the funny side joined in but Wayne and Marcus looked decidedly unimpressed. Marcus snatched the box from Wayne and stepped forward.

'*This is worthless and you ain't having it neither mister I'll burn it all, leading us on like that.*'

Like a rattlesnake hidden under a rock, Gordon produced a dagger and grabbing Marcus by his lapel pointed the sharp blade under his chin. A small trickle of blood started to run down his neck.

'*Why don't you inspect those photographs more closely they are of my wife and child who have since passed, the contents of that box is all I have to remember them by, rescind or die - your choice?*'

'*Yeah well, you can't blame us for being a bit uppity you made it sound like we were going to be set for life.*'

'No gentlemen, I said you would be rewarded and that you will. If I were to give you a penny each for your troubles I would still be in the right. I cannot be held accountable for your erroneous assumptions can I?' said Gordon pulling away the knife and releasing his grip.

'He has you there dear fellow.' said Bill straightening his cap.

'I concur, he never actually specified what the reward was, very clever old man.' said Arthur with a smile.

'You all misunderstand Gentleman this is pure treasure to me. When I lost my family I knew not how I could go on but somehow I did. All I had left of them was that precious little box. You think me a fool for leaving it unattended, but what value is that box to anyone except me?'

'*It looks like a jewellery box or sumink you bleedn idiot.*' screamed Marcus.

'My intention was not to deceive you. I am offering you a night out in the best places in London all on me.'

'So how much money have you got on ya then?' said Wayne stepping closer. Marcus stepped forward as well. The expression on their faces changing from facilitator to unwelcome villainy.

'You never thought to wonder why I would carry a gun did you lads?' said Arthur holding it in his waistband rather proudly.

Wayne looked at him quizzically. Marcus' face suddenly lit up like a man who realised he had just stepped in front of a growler.

'*You're a bloody peeler ain't you?*'

'Cor, that makes sense that's why he been leading the charge, *let's get outta ere.*' added Wayne

'Not so fast Gentleman, I see that you are rogues and you only helped for your own gain, or possibly planned to steal the treasure for yourselves, but you have aided me in restoring my precious family memories and for that you should be rightfully rewarded. I think that should cover it.' said Gordon handing them over five pounds each.

'You shall not hear from us anymore sir, that I promise.' said Wayne taking off his cap and waving it before him.

'It has been an honour, always at your service.' said Marcus straightening his messy suit and bowing down further than necessary. With that they disappeared down a well-hidden alley confident in their stride.'

'They know the Nichol then.' remarked Bill.

'Of course they do. Villains, the pair of them. Even if there were treasure in that box you would not have seen it, that I assure you, I have seen their type many a time.' said Arthur.

'I promised them a reward and they got one. A man is nothing if he cannot keep his word.' replied Gordon.

'Rather generous I would have said.' Bill remarked brushing down his hat.

'I suggest we make our getaway, we can finish our parlance once we are back in the cab.' said Arthur.

'Quite, but how do we get out of this maze?' asked Gordon looking around.

'In the corner, an alley going in the right direction.' said Bill.

'Excellent, well spotted my good man. I will lead the way.' said Gordon

The men walked briskly and managed to navigate their way back past several familiar landmarks. Upon their return to the main street they discovered both hansom's still waiting. Gordon approached the first driver and tipped him five pounds. After tipping the other driver they all boarded the same hansom back.

'Thank you kind sir.' said Gordon stepping out of the hansom.

'Well I have to say, it has been an awfully exciting adventure.' said Bill grinning.

'That it has.' replied Arthur.

'Gentleman your conduct tonight has been nothing short of spectacular as promised I shall take you out for the night of your lives on Saturday but have a drink on me in the meantime.'

'*Cor blimey that's five pounds.*' cried Bill.

'Yes, and there is more to come on Saturday night.'

'You do not need to repay us. We were glad to have helped.' said Arthur tipping his bowler hat.

'Nonsense, you have found my long lost wife. Money's not everything.'

Arthur laughed. 'Ok Gordon, if you insist.'

Bill breathed a sigh of relief.

'Well Gentleman, Saturday, seven pm sharp, on this very concourse.'

'There is one thing before you leave.' said Arthur.

'Oh, what is that my friend?' replied Gordon

'It is just that you were going away was you not? Hence your luggage being left in the station.'

Bill laughed. 'Crikey Arthur, you must be a Bobby I never thought of that and I am the porter.'

'Yes I quite agree well observed, and of course you are correct. This escapade however has changed my mind. I will return home and make my visitation another time.'

Arthur smiled and extended his hand. Gordon shook both Arthur's and Bill's hand and then lifting his hat bade them goodnight.

Gordon raced into the station and collected his luggage, then he jumped into a hansom and told the driver to go as fast he can. Once he arrived home, Gordon threw some money at the driver and ran down his garden path. He took out his key and hastily unlocked the thick wooden door; he nearly dropped his box as he shoulder barged it prematurely.

Once inside he went to his pile of old broadsheets and used some to start a roaring fire. He placed the box on his small drinks table that set next to his red leather armchair. He prepared a pipe and poured himself a whisky. He changed into his treasured red velvet robe and finally sat down placing the box in the centre of his lap. Inhaling the heavy tobacco smoke he exhaled with pleasure and allowed some whisky to leisurely slide down his throat.

He opened the box and looked through the trinkets, the ring, the earrings and the little wooden ballerina carving. The photo of the woman and child caught his eye; he pulled it out and stared at it. Then Gordon emptied everything onto the table. After inspecting the bottom of the box he pulled out a thin piece of metal from his robe pocket. He picked the box up, held it upside down and shook it. Nothing but the sound of splitting wood from the fire. Turning the box back over he carefully shimmied the metal shard in between the base and the side of the box. He slowly lifted up the false bottom.

Gordon saw the old newspaper scrunched up just as he had left it. He opened the paper up, pulled out the huge diamond and held it up to the fire. Watching a thousand flames burn before him he picked up the photo of the woman and kissed it.

'Well I do love you as well sis.' said he.

Next of Kin

The alleys of London filled with fog, dark gloom filled the day and frozen terror filled the night. The streets were empty. This was not a time to be out. In the few hours of daylight mercifully given one might venture down to the Thames and skate along its frozen face. The winter fair may have brought a day or two's respite but Christmas had passed and the long haul of January had begun.

'Nary would anyone venture out on a such a night.' the man said to himself sitting by the roaring fire in his lodgings. He had over his lap a thick blanket and clasped a hot cup of tea as if his life depended on it.

The scratch laden clock that stood on the chipped and marred mantelpiece said it was eleven, time to retire but the man could not face the prospect of an icy cold bedroom. '*Maybe I should just sleep here,*' he thought to himself.

As he contemplated the decision he allowed his head to drop slowly and his eyes to close. '*I should put the cup of tea down really.*' he idly thought to himself as the land of slumber sucked him into its inescapable clutches.

A series of really loud thuds woke him up with a jolt. The tea spilt, he realised it was still warm he could not have been asleep long. There was silence. Had he been dreaming? He gulped down his now tepid beverage. There was another loud thud. There *is* someone at the door. The man rubbed his eyes and looked at the clock; it was quarter past the hour. 'Who the devil is calling at this hour?' he muttered to himself.

The banging on the door began again in earnest.
'John, John, it's me Terrence, open up please.'

The man leapt to his feet and opened the front door.
'By Jove what are you doing here at this time of night, is your house on fire?'

'I wish it were John, I really do.'

John pulled him in by the sleeve of his overcoat. Terence did not argue but entered and walked straight up to the fire.

'Pull that chair up Terence. You are welcome to have some tea, but you can make it yourself the water may still have some warmth.'

'Something stronger perhaps.' replied Terence with a strange look of desperation in his eyes.

John stared at his interlocutor. He was not particularly surprised when he opened the door to see the face of his friend had a deathly pallor, but as his face flickered in the warmth of the fire he observed that no colour was returning and the shaking of his hands was still palpable. It crossed his mind that perhaps it was not the cold that had his friend in such a wretched physical state.

'The decanter is on the table pour yourself one.'

Terence got up and after taking a cheap looking green coloured glass poured himself a healthy measure. Instantly he took a large gulp and then topped himself up again, he looked back at his friend gesturing the glass towards him.

'No, I am fine Terence. Thank you.'

'Ok, well thank you for your hospitality.'

'Not at all.' replied John pointing his hand toward the seat that Terrence had pulled up to the fire.

'What troubles you so?' asked John looking at his friend.

Terrence looked back at him, his blonde hair became flecked gold in the firelight and his black coat glistened with dying snowflakes. 'I am afraid you would not believe me, John.'

'*Yes I would and in any case you better damn well try getting me up at this hour.*' John snapped back.

'That would be a fair statement.' Terrence said rolling the glass in his hand. 'It is a spectre.'

'*A spectre*, good heavens what do you mean a spectre?'

'A spectre, an apparition, a spirit, a ghost.'

'Where, out in the street man? In the graveyard? *Why are you waking me at such an hour, tell me in the morning, I have work on the morrow you know.*' John stared at his friend. Terrence just stared into the flames.

John exhaled deeply. 'Perhaps I will join you in a drink.' he went to rise out of his chair but Terence beat him to it. He quickly returned with a glass for John and a refill for himself.

'I assume that this more than just a random sighting.'

'You assume correct, it is in my house. *In my house.*' Terrence reiterated.

'What is man?'

'This confounded apparition that keeps on haunting me.'

'You have actually seen it?'

'Yes, tonight, but it has been building up all week. I was almost too frightened to stay there and then tonight ... that was it I was off. *I consider myself a man and I will fight but how can you fight that.*'

'Terence calm down, you are here now and you can stay the night. You will have to sleep in the chair by the fire. Now take a sip of brandy and start from the beginning.'

It all began last weekend. Things kept on disappearing. I mean inexplicably. I would put a knife down in the kitchen and it would not be there a minute later. One of my tools went missing. I was hammering a nail into some wood and I bent down to see how far it had gone through, when I looked back up the hammer was gone. Nowhere in sight.

'You must have mislaid it.'

'Confound you John, were you not listening I had just had it in my hand.'

'So where was it?' replied John calmly taking a sip of his brandy.

'Well, that is where the tale gets even stranger. Having failed to find it I had no choice but to ascertain that I myself was mistaken and that I could not have had it in my hand. I returned into the house and after checking the kitchen I went into the dining area, there laid out on display was the hammer, the box of nails and the knife I had lost earlier.

I did not even realise that the box of nails was missing you understand. Convinced that this could not be I marched back out into the garden. There right where I was working was the hammer and nails. Swiftly I turned on my heels and ran back into the dining section of the parlour. They were still on the table!

Flabbergasted, I ran back outside again. The hammer and nails were still there so I picked them up and returned inside carrying them in my hands. They were *not* on the table anymore just the knife. I ran to the front door lest someone be having a jape on me, but it was locked and fastened tight. Defeated, I scratched my head and sat down on my parlour chair with my hammer and box of nails in hand.'

'Are you sure that it was the same hammer and box of nails?'

'Of course. When a man possesses such items they bear their own marks, my hammer has a chip at the end of the wooden handle, my box of nails is ripped on the corner and has such a multitude of scratches that they would be impossible to count.'

'I agree it is peculiar.'

'Peculiar does not address it. I sat there wondering if I was losing my mind when I heard a man laugh. I leapt off the chair as the voice sounded as if it were right next to me. I grabbed my keys and ran out of the front door in such a state that I forgot to lock the back door.

I tell you John, it took me a while to summon up the courage to re-enter my premises. Leaving the front door open, I ran to the back door slammed it shut, locked it, and then fled back out of the front door violently closing it behind me.'

'What did you do then?'

'I went down the pub.'

John laughed louder than he intended.

'What else is a man to do? After the pub closed, I wended my way home a lot calmer and full of the courage that only alcohol seems to offer. I went into my house and shouted out that I would catch whoever it was. By now I was convinced it must be some fiendishly clever trick. There was no response. I went through every room, checked every corner, I even went out into the backyard. Nothing. In the Parlour, I waited a while to see if anything would happen but soon the alcohol got the better of me and I became overwrought with lethargy.

I retired to my bed and the next thing I knew it was morning. Initially, the previous day's events slipped my mind. As I breakfasted my fork stopped halfway to my mouth as yesterday's events burst forth. Apprehension crept in, but I decided that in my haste I had probably overlooked something that would have given me the answer.

As you will no doubt be aware much has been made of spirits and ghosts in the newspapers and spiritualism grows by the day. Even *Arthur Conan Doyle* is interested in it, but I have never been inclined to believe in such things and I thought there must be a simple explanation that I have overlooked. The day turned out to be perfectly normal and by the end of it I started laughing at myself for being duped.

'What about the laugh?'

'Yes, I was aware of that also. Not easy to explain away. In truth I have thought someone called my name before when they didn't so either a trick of the mind or something.'

'You no longer consider it to be a Jape?'

'Albeit it was a possibility I ended up putting the blame entirely on myself. After all, there was no sign of a break-in and everything was locked up hitherto me going out in the garden.'

'What was the next event?' John said downing the last of his Brandy, then getting up and taking Terence's glass without asking, he approached the decanter and began refilling.

'Nothing for the next day or two. I happily returned to normal life. One morning I came down and found the parlour chairs around the dining table, the dining chairs in a circle by the fire and every single piece of cutlery that I own laid out on the table.'

'*Good Grief.*'

'Yes, exactly John. The sight of it chilled my blood. If this was a Jape it was quickly becoming a serious incident. It never fails to amuse me how fickle our minds are John. I quickly became convinced this *was* the work of a poltergeist.'

'That is serious, you mentioned an apparition but I did not realise the extent of your experiences.'

'I was embarrassed John. I feared that people would laugh at me and my credibility would be ruined. You are my closest confidant John but I feared even you would sneer at me and in truth I wondered if I needed you to. After the events of tonight, I thought if you don't believe me, I will have you visit my house.

'You are a friend regardless of my personal beliefs, I believe you are earnest and that is what I expect of both a friend and a gentleman.'

'Thank you John. I cannot expect you to alter your view of the world for chosen words from an acquaintance but please allow me to continue my discourse. The odd behaviour increased you see. I went through the rituals of double checking all locks and windows, but there seemed to be only one conclusion - it was a supernatural force.' Terence put his glass down in front of the fire. He remained leant forward and looked John straight in the eyes. 'John, I would walk out of the room, come back in and the furniture would be rearranged or things would be sitting in the middle of the floor that had clearly not been there before. The clock for example; there is no rhyme or reason why it should be sitting in the middle of the parlour room floor. This was happening not two or three minutes after leaving the room you understand. Then the voice came back.'

'What did it say?' said John holding his glass ever tighter.

'It insulted and threatened me, said I would never leave this place alive and that it would haunt me until the day I die. I tried to reason with it but it would not listen. It would not even talk to me. Then it got violent, randomly throw things at me, my nerves are tattered as you can probably tell.'

'Yes, you are correct. Initially I thought it was the cold that had you so shaken but I plainly see now that it is not.'

'I tell you John you maybe coming to visit me in an asylum soon.'

'Don't be so melodramatic man, finish relaying all to me and then we shall we form a plan of action.'

'It escalated rapidly with me being abused, threatened and assaulted by a variety of flying objects. It all culminated tonight when he shouted at me to leave him alone and came flying through the wall in physical form.'

'Physical form?'

'Yes physical as in that I could bear witness to his appearance. It was transparent as you would expect.'

'Well, what did he look like man?'

'He was tall and lithe, gaunt with sunken eyes and flecked grey hair across his balding head. His nose was like a beak and he had evil beady eyes. He wore a red robe over bed clothing.'

'He looked old then?'

'Difficult to say he could be fifties, he looked strong despite his ageing appearance, it looked like he had aged prematurely.'

'What did you do Terrence?'

'What did I do? I bolted straight out of the door and ran here to you with the image of that beastly man imprinted on my mind, all I could see was him around every corner, in every alley I was sure would I run headlong into him.' Terence said in a voice laced with desperation, he leant down and picked his glass back up from the floor.

'Fair comment.' replied John.

'Apologies for putting myself upon you like this but I did not know where else to go at such an hour. Despite our apparent class difference you have proven yourself to be a most trustworthy and loyal friend.'

'Class is overrated. Men will be men, class does not distinguish good from bad.'

'A profound and sagacious statement but what am I to do about the problem at hand?'

John sat there and rubbed his chin.

'Tonight you shall remain here, you will have to sleep in the parlour of course, you may use what you will to keep yourself comfortable and of course help yourself to the brandy. Then tomorrow return to your dwelling and if it happens again message me at once and I shall come straight over.'

'Thank you so much John. I will buy you two bottles of Brandy on the morrow and not cheap stuff either.'

'That is most kind but not necessary. Tell me, is it more active at night?'

'Things occur at all hours, but at night it is particularly terrifying and that is when he usually speaks. I suspect the rascal knows the dark and gloom makes it all the more frightful.'

'I have work on the morrow so I must retire. You may let yourself out in the morning as I shall not have time to breakfast.'

'Very well John, thank you my friend.'

After work the next day John stepped into a pub and treated himself to a meal along with a few beers. The pub he liked to frequent was halfway between his lodgings and Terence's house. He planned to arrive unannounced at Terence's then wait outside to see if he could hear anything. If the spirit taunted Terrence he would be sure to run straight out of the door to which John would run straight in and catch it in the act.

He arrived at Terence's house and saw the lights were on. The road was quiet. The street lamps had been lit and in the freezing fog they looked like floating golden orbs. The air was cold, biting cold, it stung his nostrils as if he were breathing in razor blades, he rubbed his hands and put them in his pocket, moving his fingers to keep them warm and the circulation flowing. The plan had seemed so well thought out. He knew it was cold but quickly realised he had underestimated effect of it when you are standing still for a long period.

'A clacking of hooves temporarily brought the street to life as a Brougham pulled up at one of the houses down the street. John noticed a tall man with a black cloak and a top hat get out, pay the driver and enter his abode. *'Lucky devil.'* John thought to himself as he imagined a nice warm fire and a glass of brandy.

Minutes passed, he could see the lights on in the parlour and upstairs. John could feel his extremities getting colder and colder he wondered how long his vigil could continue. Perhaps this errand was a foolish one. He could be out here for hours. As the clatter of hooves gently faded away the eerie silence of a foggy London night returned.

The sound of a man screaming broke the stillness. John looked up - it had come from Terence's house.

'Leave me alone o great spectre, back to the dead with you ... please!'

'I shall never leave you alone. I am your tormentor.' a strange voice shrieked in reply.

There was a loud crashing noise as if something had been turned over.

John sprinted up the steps to the red front door. Before he could get to it Terence came fleeing out and down the stairs in such a hurry that John had to leap back to the pavement to save them both from rolling down the steps together.

'John thank mercy you are here, what timing, he has just paid me another visit, go in there and see for yourself.'

'I heard for myself Terence now pull yourself together. There's a good chap.'

'No John go in, you must enter and see for yourself, please.'

'Calm down man.' said John shaking him violently by the shoulders. 'We shall enter together and address this spectral fiend ourselves. Tonight is the last that you shall have bother with it I guarantee, now take a deep breath and calm down.' said John straightening his cap.

Terence took a deep breath and with a complexion as pale as the moon reluctantly climbed the steps alongside John. They opened the door and entered the reception room that the front door opened into.

Compared to the cheap lodgings of John the house always seemed palatial, nice paintings on the wall, china and crystal sets, expensive liquor. John paid no attention to such things today. A sideboard was upturned and he guessed that was the crash that he had heard from outside. Other than that everything was perceived to be normal. He looked behind him. Terence was standing in the corner of the room with the front door open.

'Come in and shut the door, confound you we'll freeze to death!' said John marching forward and slamming the door shut, he gently pulled Terence into the middle of the room by the sleeve of his jacket.

'Come forward O spirit so that I may have words with you.' said John.

'I knew, I knew it, he will not appear now that someone can bear witness.' cried Terrence.

'I said come forward spirit. You consider me a fool I was outside I heard everything. You do not scare me, come forward and face me if you dare.'

The furniture started to shake violently and the gas lights flickered. A deep loud voice proclaimed *'If I dare.'*

Terence grabbed John's arm and tugged it like a child desperate for his father's attention. *'What have you done John? You have angered it. Now we will face its wrath.'*

'*If I dare!*' the spectre boomed so loud that they could feel the reverberation. The door to the next room slammed opened and the spectre came flying through screaming straight towards them. Terence cowered whilst John just stood there. Terence noticed that John had no tremor of either nerves or fear.

As the spirit realised John was not going to turn and flee it stopped in front of them and rose up into the air enlarging itself, forcing them to look up at it as it towered over them. Terence could barely look.

'I think a drink might be in order. Don't you Terence?' said John as he walked calmly over to the decanter. 'You don't mind do you Terence?' said John about to pour.

'N ... n ... not at all John.' he replied finally standing up straight.

'Although it is contrary to my desires would you care to partake, o' vicious phantom?'

The malevolent spirit glared at John with its beady eyes. John stared back. The ghost lunged forward with its oversized head and screamed in his face. John stood his ground without as much as a flinch.

'Am I to take it that you decline my invitation?' said John walking across the room to give Terence his drink.

'*You think you shall not fear me, that I will not terrify, but you will you cower before me, scream my name and beg for me to end the torture, but never shall I.*'

'*Who do you address you wretched apparition? You think you can intimidate me I warn you sir it is quite the opposite if you do not watch your ways you will rue the day you met me.*' John turned to check on Terence and realised that his expression now read surprise and curiosity instead of immortal terror.

The ghost looked as equally baffled it stood there floating above them with its dirty red bathrobe and stained striped pyjamas.

'*Why do you haunt my friend so apparition?*' cried John.

'*Because I enjoy it.*' came the reply.

John took a sip of his brandy.

'*Well from this day forth you will leave him alone infernal spectre do you hear me?*'

'*Never ... no ... no ... never, your talk is nothing I am dead what can you do to me?*' As it said this it swirled around the room pulling evil faces.

'*This is your last warning o phantom.*' shouted John.

'*No it is yours!*' screamed the apparition. It surged forward and pushed Terence so hard that he flew back into the wall. Two chairs flew across the room of their own accord, one hit Terence, the other hit John but he managed to deflect it with his arms. Objects started flying around the room. Terence covered himself up using his arms to protect himself. Before John could do anything a glass smashed into the side of his head and the sideboard went flying into his chest, he flew back and landed on the floor with a heavy thud.

John looked up. The spectre was floating high in the middle of the room laughing.

'*Scared now are we sir, I told you would be.*' the phantom taunted.

John wiped his forehead and saw the blood on his hand, he felt a trickle run down the side of his face, his hair was becoming matted with blood. He realised that the glass that had hit him was a thick one.

'*And I told you sir, that you would be the one who would be petrified.*' as John said it he flipped the sideboard off him like a playing card. He jumped to his feet. '*Dave,

Dave, Dave come hither Dave the need is great, come hither now.' screamed John.

Terence unfolded his arms and got up. 'Who are you calling?'

'*Call who you want the more I can torment the better.'* said the apparition violently nudging both of them as it circled by.

'*I am calling my brother.*' said John.

'*Your brother?* I never knew you had a brother.'

There was a thud on the door; it was so loud that it startled Terence. John walked over to the door and threw it open. In walked the biggest man that Terence had ever seen. He was well over six feet tall wearing pinstriped trousers, a black waistcoat and a white shirt with the sleeves ripped off at the shoulder. His muscles bulged and he looked dirty, yet he wore a relatively clean top hat. He also had a goat-like beard. Terence kept on staring as there was something not right about John's brother but he could not place it.

John's brother Dave stood there looking at the ghost snarling.

'*Ha, what can he to do me I am dead you fool, dead.*' the spectre replied cackling.

'So is he.' replied John.

It was then that Terence realised the more he looked at Dave the more he could see through him.

'*What no, it cannot be ... no.*' the phantom's face turned to sheer terror; it ran back through the wall.

Dave ran straight after him. '*Pick on my brother, my brother ...*' the voice trailed off as he went through the same wall. A few seconds later the apparition came flying back through into the reception room with teeth flying out of its mouth. Dave ran after it and continued punching its face in.

'*No, please no. I will do anything.*' the spectral tormentor screamed.

John laughed. '*Who's terrified now?*'

Dave kicked, stamped and beat the ghost until there was almost nothing left. '*You ever come near my brother or his friend again and I will do this every day.*'

'*I won't. I promise. I promise. I promise ... I prom ...*' the ghost faded away.

Dave walked over to his brother. 'Are you alright?'

'Yes I am. Thanks brother. Be sure to come and see me soon,'

'Will do.'

'Thanks Dave.' said Terence cautiously stepping away from the sibling spectre at the same time.

'Hasn't anyone taught you not to be afraid of ghosts yet Terence? You don't need to fear me lad. Only people like that should fear me and rightly so. Just shout my name.' Dave lifted his top hat off in salute and disappeared into the floor.

'*Thank you kind sir.*' shouted Terence after him.

'Well, we better get this place tidied up and then perhaps a celebration.'

'*Celebration John we certainly shall on the morrow I am taking you out and rewarding you every way I can think of*, but for now a few drinks will have to do.'

'I accept. There is one thing I shall say for certain.'

'Oh, what is that?'

'You shan't be seeing that ghost again.'

As they righted the sideboard, Terence burst into a raucous fit of laughter.

To Stay or Not to Tay

'What the hell do you mean you didn't mean to steal it?'

'I don't know it just happened.' he shrugged.

'The Medics are the most feared gang in London.'

'*I know, I know.*'

'*You know? Then why in bloody hell did you do it for then?*'

The man in his waistcoat looked away into the head height shelf.

'*Lionel Spaldwick, I suggest you answer me.*'

'What do you want from me Anne? I didn't mean to I just saw it and took it.'

'*Why did you have to take two hundred and fifty quid for, why not just a tenner? That would have lasted us ages and they might have forgiven you.*'

He stared at her as if he were looking back at himself.

'Yeah you're right they forgive no one.' replied Anne grabbing her matted brown hair.

'I just wanted to get away from all this, to start a new life, we're never gonna amount to anything around here.'

'None of us are you idiot, oh Lionel you have really done it this time haven't you, so your solution to our poverty is to get us both killed, nice one, *bravo Lionel bravo!*' the woman said clapping sarcastically loud.

'*Well what the bloody ell ave you done to get us out of this bleedin mess eh?*' Lionel sneered.

'*Don't you talk to me like that; I'm not afraid of you.*' Anne screamed walking towards him.

'Sorry love, you know I love you, I only did it for us, if I didn't I would have been away by know wouldn't I? I want you to be my wife but I can't do that while we live in squalor can I?'

'If you want me to become Anne Spaldwick instead of Anne Millow you better get us out of this mess.'

'I will try my best, I promise.'

'Not good enough, where is it?'

'What?'

'*The money, you damn fool, where is the money?*'

'In my pocket.'

'*In your pocket* – Christ, I need a drink.' Anne said slapping her head harder than she intended.

She went out of the bedroom into their living quarters, Lionel followed. She picked up a nearly empty gin bottle and took a large gulp, she got a dirty glass and poured in another one. She sat down on a chairs that looked like it should have been thrown out twenty years ago.

'Do they know?'

Grabbing an even dirtier glass Lionel poured himself a glass of mother's ruin and sat down. He sighed heavily and his hands began to tremble slightly.

'Yes.'

'How do you know?'

'Because, on the way home someone approached me.'

'*Who? What did they say?*' asked Anne now starting to tremble herself.

'I don't know who it was but he didn't look very pleasant, all he said was that they knew what I had done and I was to return home and wait and I'd be visited shortly.'

'Oh great, so now you have brought them ere. Well I don't know you, you understand, we are not together, I am your cousin visiting from Brighton or sumink, right?'

'*It won't work Lionel.* They know everything already, it's how they work. You knew how powerful the medics were why did you get mixed up with them for?'

'Money, what the bloody ell do you think? A mate of mine reckoned he did a piece of work for em and he got good money for it, did next to nothing, he was a look out I think.'

'So why didn't you?'

'Cos the first thing they wanted me to do was help in an armed robbery, you could bloody swing for that, I told em no chance but asked if they had anything else I could do. Well the bleedin idiot said he would have a look and left the room. It was then that I noticed the cash sitting on the desk, there was a lot more than two hundred and fifty so was hoping they wouldn't miss it.

'You idiot, they wanted you take it and now you owe them you'll be robbing banks and probably end up swingin for free.'

'Oh come on every person has a heart somewhere.'

'The Dreaded Doctor doesn't everyone knows that.'

Lionel finally kicked off his worn down shoes exposing his smelly dank sock with toes sticking out like unwelcome mushrooms in a garden.

'So what do I do?'

'I don't know, it's your mess, you better bleedin sort it.' retorted Anne rolling herself a cigarette out of old stale tobacco.'

'Roll us one.'

'Roll one yourself.' she said closing the tin and throwing it into his chest as hard as she could.

'Look we need to come up with a plan we need to-'

Lionel was cut short by a loud thud at the door that slammed their hearts into their mouths.

'*What should I do?*' pleaded Lionel.

'There's no choice, if we ignore the door they'll just kick it in and there's no other way out.'

Lionel looked around the room in a panic.

'*Open up or we're comin in anyway.*' A voice yelled from behind their front door.

Anne exhaled deeply, stood up and brushed down her dirty grey dress. '*I'll go.*' she walked to the front door and swung it open violently.

'*What the hell do you want shouting like that.*' she screamed feigning complete innocence.

A large man with a bald head and thick brown coat shoved her out of the way and walked past as if she were nothing.

'*Hey, who you pushing mister?*'

She looked out into the passage. '*At least they only sent one.*' she said to herself.

The huge man was sitting in their decrepit armchair, he completely filled it, he had one foot on his other knee, his fingers were drumming the wood impatiently.

'Who are ya? Get outta my bloody house.' Anne yelled approaching him.

He did not flinch or react, in a very quiet tone he looked at Lionel and said.

'If you don't shut her up I will.'

'*For God's sake Anne keep your gob shut.*' Anne scowled at him but remained silent.

'You know who I am Lionel?'

'Not exactly but I can guess where you're from. Look I'm sorry I wasn't thinking I have never seen so much money before and you can see for yourself the squalor that we live in.'

'I should kill you and I will probably questioned as to why I didn't – if I don't that is.'

'Look I know who the medics are there is no reason I would ever steal from you I know how powerful you are.' said Lionel his quivering so visible even his locks of hair were dancing.

'But you did.' replied the man lighting a cigarette.

'*I have no idea what came over me, I'm sorry, I really am sorry.*' Lionel realised he still had the money on him and grabbed it out of his pocket, he held the sheets of paper up waving them frantically at him.

The man held his hand up refusing take it.

'*Just take it, he's got the money and no harm has been done, just take the blasted money damn you.*' screamed Anne stepping forward but making sure she did not get too close.

'If you utter another word I will kill you regardless of my decision to kill him.' said he pulling out a revolver and pointing it at her.

Her skin paled and she took a deep breath stepping back into the wall as if hoping that she would somehow pass through it.

Without a word, their visitor put the gun back in his coat and turned his attention back to Lionel, whose hand was trembling so violently that the notes were now rattling.

'I believe you Lionel but you still made a very stupid mistake, I'll tell you what I'll do. I want you to keep the two hundred and fifty pounds.'

'*No ... please.*' Lionel shrieked in a voice so high he didn't recognise it as his own.

The man held up his huge hand to silence him. 'Let me finish, you can keep the 250 pounds for now but I want it you to double it. You have seven days. It is eight pm, you have until eight pm a week today to get me 500 pounds, if you do it you I will consider your transgressions forgiven. If you cannot give me 500 then you are to return the 250 to me personally, you will then work for the medics until I deem that you have paid it all off. Considering the amount you owe, you will need a strong stomach because the jobs we're going to give you won't be pleasant.'

Lionel sat there with his hands in his face.

'You think I have been unfair?'

'*No* ... no not at all, it's just that I don't think I could do either.' replied Lionel.

'Those are my terms take them or leave them.' the man said once again pulling out his revolver.

'*I'll take 'em, I'll take 'em and thank you for not killing me.*'

'That's more like it.' he replied standing up and buttoning up his coat. 'You have a week so I suggest you get thinking, oh don't think about leaving London or we'll know.'

'What if I need to leave London to make the 500?'

The man looked with a hard stare into Lionel's brown eyes and said.

'Open a window, it stinks in here.' he said walking calmly out.

Anne ran and slammed the door shut behind him. 'What the '*ell* are we going to do now Lionel eh?'

'I don't know but at least I bought us some time.'

'Bought us some time, you cheeky bastard, you didn't buy us time, why that monster has given us a chance has nothing to do you.' Anne said sitting down pouring yet another drink.

Lionel pulled out the money. 'I can't believe that he left it with me.'

'Above everything that's what really scares me. I think they are going to kill you.'

'Don't say that Anne for crying out loud. Where's the gin?'

'Behind you and don't it drink it all.'

'*Shut up woman.*' said Lionel reaching for the bottle like a dying man reaching for his last drink of water. 'What do you think they'll make me do if I have to work it off?'

'*Lionel stop being a bloody idiot* that's what they want, they'll get you to kill someone or something, its 250 pounds Lionel not half a crown, they are hardly likely to say ok sweep up for a month and then off you go like a good boy are they?'

'I hate it when you're right.'

'What you live in eternal hatred?'

Lionel managed a wry smile; he loved it when Anne made him laugh and showed her softer underbelly that she worked so meticulously to hide from everyone. 'Very funny, what shall we do then?'

'I dunno. There is no guaranteed way that we can double that money unless we could place a bet that was guaranteed to come in.'

'There is no way of guaranteeing anything, if there was I would get us a thousand pounds let alone five hundred.'

'Isn't there anyone you know that can help us in any way, you seem to know everyone.'

'I don't.' said Lionel strolling around the room with his hands in pockets. 'There is no one in London that can help ... unless.'

'*What, what?*' shrieked Anne.

'It is a long shot but I have a great uncle who may be able to help. I haven't seen him since I was young but we are family and you never know, he may be able to double our money or even give us the money.'

'So where does he live?'

'Dundee. You know the funny thing is my cousin happened to mention him the other week and call it providence but I enquired where lived and he went into extraordinary details, apparently one of my other cousins has even been up there last year.'

'Yes, but *we can't leave London can we?*'

'Why can't we?'

'You heard what he said, don't leave London.'

'Yes, but when I said that I might leave London all he said was this place stinks.'

'*That wasn't permission you blasted fool.*'

'*Stop shouting at me woman.*' screamed Lionel at the top of his lungs.

Anne was taken aback but let out a smile that revealed the true perversity of their relationship.

'It is not much I know, but as he never actually said that I could not leave town if it was to double the money; it gives us a slight advantage.'

'How?' she replied.

'Look, we at least have some line of defence if we're caught. All we have to do is try and sneak out of London undetected. If we get caught we will just tell the truth and say that we have to leave London in order to get their money, but here comes the clever part if we are not followed then we just won't come back and we'll live a good life up there.'

'They won't hesitate to kill us.'

'I know that's why we must leave London discreetly but not too discreetly if you know what I mean.'

'And how are we supposed to do that?'

'We'll take suitcases, then we can point out if that we wouldn't take suitcases if we were trying to hide.'

'Have to say, it's a bit dodgy but it might work.'

'If you can think of anything else better please let me know.'

'Why don't we wait a few days and see what happens.'

'No, we need to go now and in full confidence we have a plan to get their money and that is the truth. That bloke, whoever he is, certainly isn't thick he'll know we're telling the truth. Besides, what if my uncle needs a couple of days to sort it all out?'

'Ok let's do it then. Shall we go right now?'

'No, tomorrow, we'll get up first thing but let's get packed now.'

'Ok darling, I do love you.' said Anne sidling up to him and holding his face in both her hands and drawing him in for a kiss. 'Gonna take me to bed tonight are you handsome?' she said with a smile that revealed her brown stained teeth, whilst twiddling her greasy brown hair.'

'If you hurry up I might.' said Lionel with a huge grin that was nearly as filthy as their stained and dilapidated bed.

That previous night they had had rough energetic sex that for all its passion and glory was surprisingly short. Exhausted, they fell asleep dreaming of being pursued and murdered like a couple of foxes on a country estate.

He stepped into the passageway and stopped, it was late in December and the cold and damp was omnipotent. The morning air however refreshed his nasal senses. He waited for Anne to come out and then pulled the door firmly shut.

'He was right you know.'

Anne looked at Lionel with a blank expression.

'This place does stink.' said he picking up his case and cautiously heading down the passage and out into the street.

The notorious London fog carpeted the streets; people vanished in swirls of mist like ghostly apparitions. Both of them looked around expecting someone to leap out a like a tiger out of long grass but no one did. Every stranger they passed seemed to inspect them as if they knew they were not supposed to be there.

'Morning.' said a man in a top hat stepping out of the fog and beaming a huge smile.

'Uh ... yes good morning to you sir.' Lionel replied louder than anticipated as he tried to overcompensate to show confidence.

Now on a smaller road they held hands despite having sweaty palms. Slow clacking hooves could be heard in the fog up ahead drawing nearer and nearer. Their hands squeezed. Lionel sighed heavily and wiped his brow, sweating despite the fact that it was cold. A lantern became apparent in the distance - a lighthouse warning ships of imminent death.

'*Stay close.*' Lionel whispered.

Another light became visible and the ghostly fog finally succumbs to the incessant force of its intruder. A large white horse came bursting out with a tall man in a cape driving the cab, he glared at them with beady eyes and then trundled on past.

'Whoa, I thought we were done for sure then.' said Anne.

'So did I. Come on let's get to the station as quick as we can.'

'*Where do you think you're going then?*'

Anne shrieked and a brief yelp even escaped from Lionel. They looked for the agitator it was a man with a liquor bottle sitting in a doorway. He looked at them with grey stubble, a glint of light caught Lionel's eye. 'Off somewhere nice eh?'

'*Piss off you bleedin pest.*' snapped Anne.

As they walked off Lionel looked back and found the man staring at him, Lionel noticed something odd about his appearance.

'That man is no vagrant, Anne.'

'What do you mean of course he was.'

'No, his boots were clean. New I think.'

'It's Christmas; someone probably treated him.'

'No, didn't you see his hand he was wearing a gold ring.'

'Was he?'

'Yes.'

'Are you sure?'

'*Of course I bleedin am.*'

'We are being followed.'

'Don't say that.'

'Just stick with the plan we are not doing anything wrong remember.'

They came out of the side road onto one of London's mains arteries, there were people milling about everywhere disappear and reappearing in the fog – more ghosts.

The smell of chestnuts floated through the fog.

'Something for ya journey madam?' said the man with a smoke streaked face.

'No, we are fine thank you.' Lionel offered politely.

Finally, they came out on to another artery and the station was in sight. They both relaxed upon seeing it.

'The station's busy already Anne; we should have been here earlier.'

'It's not my fault.'

'I never said it was. Let's just get in the queue shall we.' They stood in line nervously scanning the station for anyone looking out of place.

'*My God, look Anne*, that bloke over there on the bench pulling out a newspaper.'

'Yeah, what about him?'

'That's the same man that said hello to us this morning.'

'You're right he must have taken a cab.'

'A bit of a coincidence.' as Lionel said it the man briefly looked at them and then pulled the newspaper over his face. '*Oh, that does it let's go back home.*'

'No Lionel, no one has approached us and like you said we are doing nothing wrong.'

Their discomfort grew and they began to twitch like pets who have just disobeyed their master. Finally it was their turn.

'*Two to Dundee please.*' Anne said at an almost shouting volume.

'*Keep your voice down.*' said Lionel squeezing her arm harm.

'So that's where your going is it?' a voice said behind them, they turned around as quick as they could to see who had said it but there was too many people.

'*Who said that? Come on show yourself?*' screamed Anne.

'Stop shouting woman.' snapped Lionel with the sweat of desperation pouring down his face.

'Is everything ok Madam.' enquired the clerk putting on his uniform cap.

'Yeah, sorry guvnor. I hate it when people say things behind your back.' replied Anne straightening out her hair.

The ticket clerk looked back at her in astonishment.

'Two to Dundee please my good man and make them the best seats available.' said Lionel pulling out a note and putting it on the counter.

The man looked at them for a second as if deciding what to do and then said. 'You'll have to change trains a few times.'

'The quickest way please.' said Anne sounding as posh as she could.

The clerk looked up at the huge station clock. 'There's a train leaving in ten minutes from platform seven.'

'Excellent, thank you.' replied Lionel taking the tickets and his change.

They walked briskly to the Platform expecting to get accosted at any second. They arrived at the platform and were greeted by an inspector.

'Where are you going?'

'Dundee.' replied Lionel.

'Just the two of you?' said the conductor stroking his bushy black beard.

Lionel could feel Anne's need for another outburst rising up in her. 'Yes sir, just the two of us today, thank you.' said he.

'Ok, on you get.'

Anne did a sarcastic curtsy as she walked by.

On the train, they checked their reservation number and were glad to find that they had a table between them.

'This is nice ain't it Lionel.' Anne said leaning her hand across the wooden table for his.

'Yes, I couldn't resist but we have to pay this money back.'

'We'll be alright love, we've made it this far, it's about time our luck changed, we might even come back with more money than we have to pay.'

'Don't forget how serious this is Anne if this doesn't work we are screwed, as in dead.'

She withdrew her hand.

Lionel looked at her and motioned with his hands to keep an eye around. The train pulled out of the station hissing and puffing angrily like a defiant dragon.

'I have never been out of London you know.'

'I know.' said Lionel reaching forward and taking her hand again. 'You're about to see the whole country now.'

She smiled and albeit her teeth were disgusting, he had long since forgotten, as his teeth were no better. Lionel adored her smile and it reminded him of his love for her. He smiled back.

'So where do we change Lionel?'

'We go through Derby and York and then change at Edinburgh to Dundee.'

'What time will we get there?'

'About seven or eight I reckon.'

'I just thought we will be up there for New Years Eve.'

'We may just be, we will get to see in a new decade in Scotland.'

'I wonder what the 1880's will be like?'

'Let's hope we find out.' replied Lionel looking out the window.

'I am going to use the ladies water closet, where is it?'

'At the end of the carriage, just carry on walking.'

As she left Lionel found himself drumming his fingers wondering why did not think to buy a newspaper or a book as it was a long journey to have with your thoughts.

Anne returned looking shocked, her complexion was pale and she was shaking slightly.

'What on earth is the matter with you.'

'The t ... t ... toilet, there was message in the toilet.'

'*What to you?*'

'It didn't say my name but I got the message.'

'What message?'

'It was written on the mirror, '*you were told not to leave London,*' tell me that was not for us?'

'It was for us it had to be.' Lionel looked around the carriage there were other couples and businessmen, everyone seemed to going about their business. A man in a grey suit was looking out of the window he turned his gaze back into the courage and looking Lionel straight in the eye. Lionel gulped and slid back down the seat.

'Perhaps we should get off at the next station?' said Anne

'That's what I was thinking, but why have they allowed us to leave?'

'What do you mean?'

'Why haven't they killed us?'

'I don't know, maybe it wasn't for us.'

'*It is a hell of a coincidence if it wasn't.*' replied Lionel.

'There's an inspector coming.'

Lionel pulled out their tickets and waited.

'Are you sure that's what it said?'

'*Of course I'm bloody sure, I'm not mad you know go and see for yourself if you don't believe me.*' shrieked Anne.

'Tickets, please.' said the Inspector.

Lionel looked up and was surprised to see it was the same man who had sold them the tickets back at the station.

'But you sold them to us.'

'Just doing my job.' he said with a blank look on his clean shaven face.

Anne withdrew a heavy bounty of air, but Lionel held up his finger to silence her outburst.

'There you go.' said Lionel handing the tickets over.

The inspector marked the tickets and gave them back. 'On the run are we?'

Anne and Lionel looked at each other.

'We are on holiday can't people have a holiday anymore?'

'You have forgotten to tie the latch on one end of you case is all.' he replied darting his eyes onto one their cases.'

'Oh yeah, I thought you were implying we were vagrants of some kind for a minute.'

'Not at all sir, enjoy the journey.' he said turning around and heading to the next customer.

Before Anne could say a word Lionel got up and walked to the back of the train. He went into the toilet and checked the mirror. There was no writing but there was a big black smudge as if someone had wiped a dirty cloth or sleeve across it.

'What colour was the writing?' asked Lionel.

'Black, why?' replied Anne looking relieved that Lionel had returned to his seat.

'Just checked the bathroom, it has been wiped off, I don't like this I feel like everyone is watching us, someone or everyone on this train is a medic I know they are.'

'I'm scared, why didn't they just shoot us on the way to the station? Do you think they are intimidating us to go back?'

'It's not there style they do not need to be so subtle.'

Apprehension and the passing countryside lulled them into a depressive slumber.

The rattling of crockery awoke Lionel with a start.

'It's ok they are serving dinner.' said Anne.

They were served several plates of stew , there was meat, vegetables and potatoes in floating in gravy.

'This is lovely thank you very much, ooh I feel proper posh now.' Anne said as the man walked back down the carriage.

The man in the uniform returned, he had already spilled some stew on his waistcoat. He placed two beers in front of them. 'Enjoy your meal.'

'Thank you sir.' replied Lionel picking up his knife and fork.

'That's a good bit of meat that is Anne.'

'Yeah the potatoes ain't bad either.'

Lionel picked up his beer, he had a dry thirst that only a long sleep can bring, he guzzled half it down. As he returned to his cutlery he gazed out the window at the passing countryside.

'Look at sky she looks angry.'

'Yeah it is a bit stormy isn't it, it'll probably rain.'

As she said it flecks of rain began hitting the window.

'Well done Anne you had to say it didn't you.'

'It's not my fault the weather's orrible anyway who cares let's enjoy dinner.'

They resumed eating as they neared the end Lionel noticed Anne swirling her knife in the remaining gravy.

'What's wrong with you?'

'There's something in this gravy.'

'What do you mean there's something in your gravy it probably a piece of meat.'

'No, it's ... it's a piece of paper.' replied Anne sliding it out with her knife. Instantly the blood drained from her face and she started shaking.

'What on earth's the matter?'

'There is something written on it.'

'What?'

'Look.'

She laid out the gravy-covered note on the table it read:

'*You were told not leave, now you will never be safe.*'

'What are we going to do Lionel? They're going to kill us on this train.'

'No, we are safe whilst we are on this train I imagine. Idiots, I told him I might have to leave town.'

'This is your fault you had to be a smart arse didn't you.'

'There is no point getting angry at me now Anne. You went along with it.'

'It must be the server who put the note in.'

'We don't know that. Look, the plates have the table numbers etched into them. A passenger could have slipped it in.'

Lionel looked around the carriage everyone was dressed smart and genially chattering away. Anne stacked their plates, mopped up the gravy with a napkin and put the note in her bag for safe keeping.

'Where are we anyway?'

'We had just left Derby when you awoke.' replied Anne.

'Confound it! I never realised that I slept for so long.' he said pulling his timepiece out and looking at it. 'Let's just keep our heads down.'

Lionel and Anne stared out at the ever-worsening weather. The server came round offering dessert but the pair could not face the possibility of another terrifying note or event.

They both tried to sleep and forget about their troubles but could not manage it. Telepathic glances were exchanged as they screamed for help from the bottom of their souls.

'It's a shame we can't answer the note.'

'Yes it is.' replied Lionel allowing his head to rattle on the window and shake his voice. 'Anne that's brilliant. What a great idea.'

'What?'

'We'll answer the note. They left us one on the toilet mirror so let's leave them one back.'

'That is a great idea. What shall we put?'

'Mmm ... let's put - we have left London to get your money will return in a couple of days.'

'Perfect. Who should go?'

'I'll have to Anne it's too dangerous for you to leave your seat.'

Lionel put his bowler hat on a got up and slowly walked to the toilet at the end. It seemed that every table he walked past was full of spies and assassins - a carriage full of death wishers waiting to make their move.

Entering the toilet he looked at the stained mirror, he began to write and was pleased to see that the smudge was big enough to leave a clear message in it. He did not alter from what he and Anne had discussed. As soon as the message was written, he returned to his seat and surreptitiously wiped his finger on the dark red upholstery as he sat down.

Another hour passed. Anne was facing the toilet.

'A lot of people are going in there Lionel.'

'We will just have to check it before we get off. It can't be much longer until we get to York.'

'We will be arriving in York within ten minutes ladies and gentleman.' the conductor announced fifteen minutes later.

Without a word, Lionel got up and walked to the toilet.

'Well?' enquired Anne as Lionel sat back down at the table.

'It has been rubbed off.'

'That's it, no message at all.'

'No.'

The train started slowing down and the wind and rain were in fierce competition to see who cause the most disruption. Anne put her green bonnet back on her head and picked up her bag. Lionel was in the aisle waiting.

The Train pulled in bellowing clouds of grey cigar smoke. They alighted and upon seeing a station porter, approached him.

'Which one is the Edinburgh train my good man?'

'Platform two, right in front of you.'

They hurried across the platform. As they were about to get into the car Anne tugged urgently on Lionel's sleeve.

'Look over there. At the man behind us.' said Anne flicking her head.

'What man?'

'*Him, look*, it's the man from Kings Cross earlier.'

Lionel looked closely. It was the same man that they had seen on the concourse, the man with the top hat, that had bade them good morning, and he was getting on to the same train.

'*He has followed us the whole way.*' shrieked Anne.

'Come on let's get on the train.'

They climbed aboard and despite being first class it was nothing compared to the newly introduced dining carriage that had he been sitting in before. The train pulled off and they watched the large station and its cavernous sheds pass by.

Lionel wished that he never knew of the power that the medics had over the whole of Victorian London. Anne saw their corpses lying by a railway track with their brains blown out, a passing warning for the locals perhaps, did the Dreaded Doctor run the whole country now? The weather seemed to match their emotions, the worse they felt, the worse the weather got, the wind began to howl like some lost wolf alone in the wilderness crying out to an empty void that would never respond.

As they pulled into Edinburgh, there was a huge crack of thunder, rain started lashing against windows. The train pulled up under the protection of the station canopy. Anne and Lionel watched the passengers trading places. The man with the top hat they had seen that very morning, walking in the opposite direction, then at Kings Cross station, the man that had followed them all the way to York was standing in front of the carriage window taunting them. He smiled and waved goodbye. Another crack of thunder made it all the more ominous. Lionel went to leap out his seat but Anne gave him the look and he sat back down. The man walked off and out of their sight.

For a minute they nervously watched the end of the carriage for fear that he might burst in and shoot them dead there and then but he never appeared. A few minutes later they were once again pulling out of the station, the rain was still lashing down and the wind was blowing so hard the windows were starting to rattle.

'This weather is ghastly. Are we going to be ok?'
Another crack of thunder.
'Of course we will be it's only a bit wind and rain.' replied Lionel looking out of the window.
'Seems awfully strong.'
'We're up north now Anne they're used to it ain't they. It's probably a nice day to them.'
'Do you think they'll kill us when we get off at Dundee.'
'I don't know.'
'Perhaps we should have got off at Edinburgh.'
'Are you serious, you saw that mad man outside the window didn't you?'

The wind charged at the train like an injured rhino, the whole carriage rocked and the windows threatened to implode. Lightning streaked across the furious sky with the roar of thousand dragons and rain smashed against the glass like bullets from a machine gun. The train slowed down and stopped.

Lionel desperately looked out the window trying to see through rain, he caught a glimpse through the deluge it was just grass and bushes.

'This isn't a station, why have we stopped?' said Lionel.

'It's the weather I told you.' replied Anne.

'They wouldn't stop us in the middle of nowhere would they.' as Lionel said that the train moved off again and started picking up speed, as if by divine intervention, the wind literally blew the rain away and what Lionel saw shocked him to the core.

They were high above water, a raging sea of venomous tide, the lightning cracked harder than a ringmaster with his whip, thunder screamed with a vengeful cry, wind smashed at the bridge with angry punches, the carriages rocked violently.

Anne gasped as she looked across the sea. 'What the hell is that? The Atlantic?'

'No you bleedin idiot it must be the river Tay, the estuary where the river meets the sea, my cousin told me about it, I bet we stopped for the bridge master.'

'*That is no bloody river.*' Anne cried as the carriage rocked with such violence that passengers had started holding on. Lightning struck the bridge. '*Look at the size of them waves they are bigger than a house.* I am telling you Lionel that last gust rocked the bridge itself.

Lionel stood up to get a better view and saw the other passengers starting to get uncomfortable. Another gust hit the carriage and Lionel nearly fell over but a second punch from the clouds put him to the floor. He looked up and there standing above him was a train attendant with a plate in his hand.

'*Dundee Cake?*' he said beaming a huge smile eerily akin to the one that the man on the platform in Edinburgh had given them. Lightning hit the bridge illuminating the sinister smile. Fright leapt into Lionel's heart, he got up and grabbed the server by the throat. The man buckled instantly falling backwards.

'*What are you waiting for? Just kill us, kill us, stop messing about, we told you what we were doing, if you don't like it kill us, kill us damn it or we'll kill you.'* Lionel screamed with his face turning red.

Lionel let go of the man and grabbed his suitcase, *'Anne get your suitcase now.'* he barked. Anne collected her case and bag and followed Lionel to the end of the carriage.

'The man is a complete and utter lunatic.' He heard the attendant say as their fellow passengers helped him back up.

Lionel and Anne stood at the end of the carriage right at the very back of the train, they saw the train attendant briskly walking the other way.

'As soon as we get to the station we jump off this train and run for our lives.'

'Ok Lionel let's do it. We'll pretend it is an emergency or something.'

The wind jolted the carriage with such force they thought it would derail. Lionel went to the door and pulled the window open. The wind it was so strong that it took his breath away; after a deep breath he looked back out.

'Please God, No!' Lionel screamed in absolute terror. *'The bridge is collapsing, come on Anne we have to jump.'*

'What?' Anne shrieked.

'Now! We have to try and make it through the girders.'

Anne looked and could see a portion of the bridge falling into the immense waves up ahead. The section they were on was now starting to collapse as well.

The brakes slammed on, they were jolted violently in the wall, Lionel kicked the door open, the girders were passing at a slower rate, the carriage started to shake violently. The sky gave a victory dance as lighting literally ripped open the heavens and thunder bellowed the cry of a fallen planet.

'Now!' he cried.

The mighty waves rose up to meet them as they fell through the air, the shock of cold water hit them instantly and they gasped life saving breaths. The train was on fire and tumbling into the sea; carriages following one by one like cattle into a slaughterhouse. There was a huge explosion as train and bridge tumbled into the water. The screeching of twisting metal pierced the night and the thunderous clang of iron versus steel fought mightily with the roaring sea.

'*Look out.*' cried Lionel as their carriage came crashing down into the water Lionel raged against the water to get next to Anne before the water carried them further apart.

'*Ahhhhhhhhhh.*' screamed Anne at the top of her lungs. Lionel looked up and saw the bridge collapsing on top of them. He tried to pray but the sea would not let him, constantly filling his mouth and face with water, it was too late the medics didn't need to kill them now, the Tay bridge would finish them instead, surely the medics didn't control the water as well?

He managed to snatch that last absurd thought as the bridge fell on top of them. They were to die he had finally accepted it. At least they wouldn't have to worry about the future. There was only one problem they were not dead, they looked at each other in the water, Anne was still wearing her green bonnet which should have been hilarious but it wasn't.

The girders had fallen all around in a rhombus.

'*It missed us, it missed us.*' cried Anne.

'*Keep hold of your suitcase or you will be sucked down.*' shouted Lionel.

The depths sucked at their feet as all the metal sunk beneath them but it was not enough to pull them under.

'Come on, let's try and get to shore.' said Anne looking toward the shore that they had left from as it was the closest.'

'No Anne we must try and make the other shore, trust me.'

'But it's cold.'

'Not as cold as you think, the sea takes many months to cool down, we can survive it.'

A huge crack of lightning lit up has face as he said it.

'What about all those other poor people?'

'They're gone, there's nothing we can do now.' said Lionel finally managing to reach her.

The pair used the cases as giant floats and kicked with all their might. They got into a rhythm and managed to use the waves to aid their progression, they would sidle up one side and go down another, moving diagonally so that they were slowly inching their way across.

Lionel realised this must be how a whale felt living its whole life gasping for air. For every breath he took another was taken away from him by either the fierce wind or a hug gob of saliva from the North Sea. Lionel and Anne bobbed up and down like a pair of puppets on an ocean string.

They slowly moved away from the disaster site and toward the other shore.

'Look.' cried Lionel, pointing at the tiny glimmer of lights as boats made their way to the disaster site. It was many exhausting hours later that the Tay Estuary finally grew board of playing its game and spat them ashore.

They lay on the stone beach, exhausted, frightened yet excited. Lightning was still roaring across the sky, the tremendous waves that had just given birth to them looked once again fascinating as if it were privilege to behold such a spectacle of nature. Both of them were shivering uncontrollably.

'Come on Anne we can't lie here.' he said grabbing her arm.

'Ow! that hurt you brute.'
'Come on into them trees over there.'

It was a small copse but for them it was perfect, there were some bushes as well that would help shelter them from the wind and rain. They could just see the huge angry waves now passing by in salute.

'We need to get warm Anne or we could die. Take your clothes off.' said Lionel hurriedly stripping himself. Anne did not argue and tore her clothes off as well. They hugged, pulling their naked bodies as close as they could, pressing into each other trying to stoke their internal furnaces.

Lionel pulled his case toward him. 'If these cases were floating they cannot be full of water let's just hope that some of our clothing is dry.' he opened it. *'They are dry. All of our clothes are dry!'*

'What do you mean they're dry? They can't be dry.' replied Anne opening her own case. *'So are mine.'* she yelled with excitement.

Once in dry clothes they beamed like school kids who had received a pair of whipping tops for Christmas. They bush they nestled in offered surprising protection; their teeth finally stopped chattering.

'Lionel, the money will be wet. What if it is unusable?'

'Anne before we left this morning I put ten pounds in my wallet?'

'So?'

'Do you know where I put the rest?'

Anne looked at him. 'In your case?'

'Exactly.'

She threw herself at him and kissed him passionately.

'All we need to do now is find your Great Uncle.'
'You don't get it Anne do you?'

'Get what?'

'We're dead.'

'Don't be so bloody stupid we're alive on this beach.'

'No honey, we're dead.' he said cupping her face. Lionel watched as her eyes lit up like the train engine exploding.

'*Of course we are, we're dead, we're dead, we have no more problems, we have the money, we even have our belongings.*'

'We just need to ensure no one think we are survivors from that train.'

'Look Lionel, the storm is breaking. Let's watch the sunrise and then go.'

'I think we should skip the nearest town and find one farther away to plan our next move?'

'What shall we say if anyone asks about our cases?'

'Don't say we're on holiday. Say ... I'm a travelling salesman and you are my assistant.'

'A great idea, well done Lionel, that's exactly what we'll say.'

The weather calmed and the rain stopped. The couple walked out onto the shoreline, sat on the beach and watched as the waves lost their anger. With immense effort, the sun cracked through and they felt its warmth on their now dry skin. As Anne watched, another solar searchlight tore through the clouds, the beam swathed across the choppy bay and she wondered whether God was collecting the souls of those on board.

Anne leaned in and kissed Lionel's arm.

'So where shall we go now?'

'You remember I said my cousin does a lot of work for rich people?'

'Yes. Why?'

'Well he overheard a professor talking about some undiscovered island off of the outer Hebrides. Only a handful of people know about, it is supposed to be a paradise and one couple has made it work already.'

'Then we shall as well my love.' Anne replied with the sun shining on her face.

How about another **VICTORIAN ADVENTURE STORY?**

Simply join my mailing list and you will be sent a link to collect your FREE Victorian Adventure Story: Rustic Universe
Don't delay sign up now
www.jon-jon.co.uk
or
http://eepurl.com/c-06wH

If you enjoyed **VICTORIAN ADVENTURE STORIES**

Why not leave a review?

To find my book on Amazon – search
B0722N94L9

http://www.amazon.com/dp/B0722N94L9

http://www.amazon.co.uk/dp/B0722N94L9

or follow the link from my website

www.Jon-Jon.co.uk

Tiger! Tiger! Tiger!

My Debut Adventure Novel Out Now!

'Fantastic Read!'
'Killer Twist!'
'Characters are Great!'
'Fully Recommend this Book!'

In an unforgiving jungle the question of Man vs Beast is about to be answered once and for all ...

Colonial India, a land that attracts hunters such as Charles, a man obsessed with killing the tiger that had long evaded him. With a team of friends and a skilled shikari he pursues his striped tormentor. But the King of Cats is no easy foe. As the jungle dances with war and world's collide will the King of the Cats triumph or will man have his way?

GET YOUR COPY NOW!

http://www.amazon.com/dp/B0722N94L9

http://www.amazon.co.uk/dp/B0722N94L9

The Jellyset Kid

Meet Warwick, a young boy who after drinking unset Jelly awakes to discover it has set *into* his body giving him superhero like abilities. Struggling to keep his powers a secret whilst trying to win the heart of Faustine, he begins to battle the bad guys but is he the only one out there with superpowers?

www.Jon-Jon.co.uk

Aaron the Alien
Rock of the Gollanollarots

In Rock of the Gollanollarots, Timmy is enlisted to help Aaron find a friend who has gone missing on the planet Nollarot

Upon discovering a barren world has replaced the once vibrant colourful planet Aaron and Timmy are soon confronted by a terrifying race of unstoppable monsters that have turned the place into a desolate rock wasteland. Held captive they must try to escape.

Can Aaron and Timmy escape their captors? What has happened to the planet Nollarot and the Gollanollarots who lived on it? Where is their friend? Can they survive long enough to unravel the mystery?

The terrifying truth is worse than they could ever have imagined ...

Sequels

The Mysterious Murder of Mr Milkzilkerdilk Zooboogadoog!

Prequel

Welcome to Bejjerwejjertejnej

www.aaronthealien.com

Contact Jon-Jon via the following details

Email: JonJonWriting@yahoo.co.uk

www.Jon-Jon.co.uk

www.AarontheAlien.com

www.twitter.com/JonJonWrites

www.Facebook.com/TigerNovel

www.Facebook.com/AarontheAlienBook

Printed in Great Britain
by Amazon